To Jeffrey —
Best wishes
Jacqueline

GW01458193

BOTTLES and POTS

by

Jacqueline Pye

For John

CONTENTS

The Enemy .. 4

When Virtue Turns to Vice .. 7

Graffito 14

Tonic 15

Mail 15

Coming to Terms 16

Cobwebs 23

St Anselm's Day 27

The Stones, The Stones .. 30

Ripples 38

The Game 39

Leaving 49

Ugly Duckling 50

Sandcastle 65

Bottles and Pots 66

The Disappointing Tale of Sour Peter 74

Retribution 78

Rocket 81

The Yellow Satchel 83

Acknowledgements 90

THE ENEMY

The word that means a fear of clowns is 'coulrophobia'.

I know this because I read it in a book given to me last year for my eighth birthday. Didn't need to look it up – you could tell from the text and it made me feel sick. I never liked clowns, ever since we were at the circus when I was very young, and one pretended to throw a bucket of water over me when it was only pieces of paper. They are the enemy now.

When I'm being naughty, my brother Jack says, "Don't be such a *clown*", because he knows I don't like that at all. Our parents usually laugh.

Jack was excited when he knew it was nearly the circus in our town. He wanted to go – begged, did extra chores, and saved up the money from his paper round. Dad eventually agreed – I think he was always going to, but wanted Jack to feel he had earned it. I really, really didn't want to go but Mum was away and I couldn't stay home alone.

The circus was pretty much the same as usual; as well as the big top, there were lots of stalls selling hot dogs, burgers or candy floss, lots of ways of winning prizes, and some pretty weird people wandering around in horrid outfits chatting to children.

"Could we go home now please?"

Jack gave me a push and said, "Don't be a misery. We only just got here."

He had a go at the tombola and won a key fob. I wanted to try for a huge stuffed giraffe, but Dad said no-one ever wins those. Then, as I turned away, out of the corner of my eye I caught sight of someone standing close by. One of those scary clowns, and he was looking in my direction. Watching me. Whitened eyes with a black cross over each, a round red nose, and a painted on smile although he himself wasn't actually smiling.

4

I asked Dad for money for a burger, and slipped away to escape from the enemy. As I paid and squirted ketchup on the burger, a hand on my shoulder made me jump.

"Hello. I saw you looking at that lovely giraffe. You liked him, I could tell."

"Yes, sir, I did. But now I have to get back to my Dad."

"I won a giraffe earlier today, but I don't really want him. Would you like him?"

All my instincts were to run. I couldn't see my family but I knew roughly where they were. Yes, I'd been told about strangers, and this clown was certainly strange. But with all the people milling around, there didn't seem to be much stranger danger going on. So I followed.

At a small, grubby caravan the clown stopped and opened the door. The paint was peeling off and the handle was all rusty. I stopped and glanced around.

"Come on in. You'll just love him. Look, there he is."

And there he was, a beautiful stuffed giraffe, nearly as tall as me. I put my hand out to stroke his long neck, and the clown took hold of my fingers. I pulled my hand away and he closed the caravan door.

"Don't rush away, dear. Won't you tell me your name?"

"I'm not allowed."

"But it's very rude not to answer."

I looked around frantically and saw a bread knife within reach on the drainer, next to some dirty cups and plates.

"I'll tell you if you turn away. I'm shy about things like that."

The clown chuckled. "How sweet," he said, and turned.

The next moment he cried out, and then there was blood surging from his back and all over my hands. Luckily not my blue dress or my new white shoes, just my hands. Now he was on the floor, making an ugly gurgling noise just for a few moments, and once he went quiet I washed myself clean. His make-up was on the table, and I picked out the fat red lipstick, wiped the 'smile' from his face with a cloth and drew a sad mouth in its place. Then I stepped over him and let myself out onto the grass and into the sunshine.

"Attention please. A young girl has gone missing. She's wearing a blue dress and white shoes. If anyone sees here, please take her to the first aid stand."

I found my way there before anyone recognised me, and Dad hugged me while Jack muttered, "Glad you're OK and everything."

Dad said I'd been naughty to be gone for so long, and that our mother would be cross when she found out. I didn't mind about that; I'd got my own back on the enemy once and for all, and felt certain they wouldn't come after me again. And I know that coulrophobia is a waste of effort – after all, now they're more afraid of us than we are of them.

WHEN VIRTUE TURNS TO VICE

You know what's really aggravating? When you take the trouble to park legally then walk to the bank, while other people simply stop on the double yellows.

A convent education can do that to a girl. You grow up polite, law-abiding, always standing back for someone in a doorway, in a supermarket aisle or in the bus queue. Never dropping litter, and even picking up bits and pieces that other people have just dropped. Occasionally I've made a show of it to try and shame them, but I just risk getting a kick or worse. At least the 'f' word can't physically hurt.

As you get to adulthood, resentment can build up. I mean, why am I so proper when it always costs me, and other people gain an advantage? Once in a while, you want to strike back.

Anyway, it was the double yellows thing that started it all. I decided that, for the next seven days, I would move over to the dark side and see what it was like to break the rules. Hopefully I'd be able to pull it off, and it'd help to get the resentment out of my system.

Day One
A bit short of cash, I drove to the bank at a quiet time and, heart rate quickening, parked right at the ATM. Couldn't help glancing around to check there was no-one nearby, then did the business. Jumped back in the car and drove at 38mph *in a 30 limit*. It felt good. The sky didn't fall in.

Day Two
Went for a walk. Dropped by the local garage and bought a paper, but grabbed a triple Bounty bar and slipped it into my pocket while in the queue. No-one noticed. Once I'd

eaten all three of the bars, I screwed up the wrapper and chucked it onto the pavement, even though there was a bin just a couple of yards away.

Passing by an especially manicured garden, I reached into the hydrangea bush (hate hydrangeas, particularly the blue ones) and snapped off a stem. Left it with its head poking out of the drain.

For most people, this sort of thing would hardly register. For a lifelong goody-two-shoes, though, it caused a modest adrenaline rush. My final bash of the day – hold the front page - was to stuff a handful of used plastic bags into the recycling bin. *No plastics*.

Day Three
Drove to the car park in town. A woman offered me her unexpired parking ticket and I took it. Strolled around the mall and into the jewellers – bright lights, glittering silver and gold, and a rotating stand with necklaces and rings, each in a velvet display box. I imagined all of the expensive stuff would be protected, but a dress ring with lots of tiny imitation diamonds just sparkled at me and I picked it up. The two assistants were both busy with customers, so I eased the ring out of the box, slipped it onto my finger, replaced the box and kept my hand in my pocket. Nothing happened.

At this point I thought it might be time to reconsider my plan. So far, what had I gained? A triple Bounty, evading a car park charge, and a sparkly ring. Total value about £35. I could quit while I was, quite literally, ahead, and I might well have if it had not been for the cashier who later mistakenly gave me too much change.

Now in the past, I always came clean when this happened. Maybe they would have had to make up the shortfall themselves, but now I thought more likely not, providing it didn't happen too often. The big companies could easily afford these things. So when the checkout woman gave me change for £20 when I'd given her a ten-pound note, I said nothing.

Two things I haven't mentioned yet: first, I have a desk job. Although it doesn't pay that much, I can just afford to run a car and you couldn't say I was anywhere near the breadline. And second, I work in a town bar three nights a week and get paid formally *and* pay the tax. I'm good at mental maths, know the prices of all the drinks, and always give punters the exact right change even when they're too far gone to notice. Always *did*, that is. Tonight, I decided to use a con that I'd read about but never thought of trying until now. The trick is, just before you take the change from the till, you dip your fingers in a nearby bowl of water so that the coins are damp when you hand them over. Because that's unpleasant, the customer pockets the coins quickly without counting them. Adding up in my head over the evening, my 'tips' came to about £29. Not bad on top of the basic pay.

I was beginning to wonder whether I'd get away with it all week, and then what it would be like to return to what was 'normal' for me.

Day Four
During the drive to work, I left my mobile on. It signalled a text coming in. I picked it up to read it, missed a traffic light changing, and nudged into the offside of another car going from left to right.

The damage was quite minor, but not surprisingly the driver was hopping mad. There seemed to be no witnesses staying to get involved, so I thought quickly and accused the other driver of cutting a red light. We argued, and he was so mad that he went to give me a slap. I kicked him hard in the groin – you never forget a self-defence class, I find. While he was catching his breath, I jumped into my car, reversed a couple of yards and sped off.

Day Five

Was wondering whether it would be wise to tell the cops about yesterday, but if they believed the other driver and if he'd taken my number - then it could cost me a lot more than I've made during my week so far. Decided against.

In the bar that night, I casually asked around the regulars whether they knew anyone who could fix my front bumper and lights quickly and cheaply. Eventually one guy said he did, but added that it would cost me. He made a call. Turns out this was the fringe of the local 'network', and I didn't like the look of the man who turned up and bought me a drink.

The deal was, he would get my car back in shape if I would look after something for him. I asked what, and he scowled. Just personal stuff, he said. Only be for a day or two. In the spirit of the experiment, I agreed and made arrangements for 'someone' to deliver the package and pick up my car the next day. During the evening there was a match on Sky Sports on the bar's TV; the place was packed and, all told, I pocketed about £36 between legitimate tips and using the damp coins con.

Just before bed, I looked hard into the mirror. My face, the same that had been so honest for so many years, was looking strangely hard. Like a gambling addict, I told myself that it would stop once my week was up and I'd got my own back on all those people who broke the rules while I'd kept them so strictly.

But the next few hours were to put paid to that.

Day Six

First thing, a couple of lads turned up at my door. The sort you wouldn't want your daughter bringing home. They asked for my car keys for the repair, and handed me a package a little smaller than a shoebox. They recommended putting it somewhere safe, leaving it unopened they stressed, and waiting for them to collect it. They couldn't say when that would be, but soon, and the car would be returned as good as new in a couple of days with no questions asked. I put the 'goods' on top of my wardrobe at the back, well out of sight.

When I got back from work, 5.30 as usual, there was a police car a few spaces down the road. A guilty conscience made me nervous. As I went in, two police – one male, one female, came up the path and stopped me from closing the door. They had a dog, one of those spaniels. You can guess what happened next – bloody dog.

In the kitchen, as they started the "I'm arresting you for ..." speech and I backed towards the worktop, a fit of madness made me pick up a small knife from the block. In an instant my arm was being wrenched up behind my back and the knife was on the floor. I started to mutter that I didn't mean to do that, I was just frightened, but clearly it didn't make an impression. They took the knife, along with the package, though I swore, truthfully, that I had no idea what was in it.

With all of this 'bad girl' stuff, the one thing that I hadn't been able to bring myself to do was to actually lie. With a few moments in the interview room to think up a strategy while I waited for the duty solicitor, I decided that I could safely give the facts as they were. Without any previous, they might be willing to believe that I didn't know for sure what was in the package, and no money had changed hands. I could still get away with it.

They grilled me about the man in the bar and about the two lads. I gave general details but nothing that would specifically lead them to any one person. I wasn't that crazy. The solicitor seemed to think it'd be all right in the end, probably a fine and a severe warning. They bailed me, anyway, but I had to find my own way home.

Late in the evening, a van drew up outside the house. Like a bad movie, two men I didn't recognise

11

shoved open the front door, found me in front of the TV, and stood very close. They smelled of stale smoke. They told me to fetch the box, and I had to admit what had happened to it. Then things got nasty: one demanded to know what I'd told the police. That should've satisfied them, but unluckily for me they didn't believe a word of it. They started to make threats and one put his hand in his pocket. I looked around wildly for something to use, picked up the near-empty red wine bottle and smashed the bottom of it on the coffee table, leaving me holding a lethal jagged, solid piece of glass.

The nearest thug lunged towards me, and I rammed the bottle into his face. Blood spattered all over and he staggered backwards screaming and clutching his face. Just for a moment I froze when I saw what I'd done, and the other man stared at me in disbelief. He grabbed his mate and dragged him from the room and out of the house. I was left with bloodstains on the carpet, on my clothes, and all over the bottle. It took me more than an hour and all of my cleaning stuff to deal with the mess.

Day Seven

Had to walk to the shops for some more carpet cleaner; faint spots could still be seen. With the small knife missing from the block, I took the next smallest and stowed it in my sleeve against my left lower arm using two rubber bands. I had the feeling, expectation even, that someone would have something to say about the glassing. Wished I had a gun; I'd never even *seen* a real gun, let alone held or used one, but I was sure I'd manage.

I didn't see it coming. A car drove alongside me – not a long, black, Mafia type, just a small, familiar van – and slowed down. The nearest window was wound down. There was a sudden movement, and an acid bomb was hurtling towards my head. I screamed as the acrid fluid started to trickle down my face, but fell silent as it took with it my eyelids and flesh from my cheeks and mouth, and settled on my sweatshirt to soak through. I had never felt such pain.

Locals looked on in horror, I imagine – couldn't see them. Someone came with a bucket of water, laid me on the pavement and poured the water over my head, face and neck and cut through the sweatshirt. Stupidly I remember thinking the water was very cold as I passed out.

The police came to the hospital. My face and eyes were bandaged and I'd been warned that there would probably be no sight left, so I said, "Sorry, I can't see you now." No-one laughed except me.

*   *   *   *   *   *

So the week did not go quite as intended. And the master plan to return to the 'normal', socially responsible lifestyle was never, after all, going to happen. I recovered a small degree of vision in my left eye, but despite repeated surgery to restructure my face, I shall always be stared at by other people, especially young children, and I don't care to look in the mirror more than I have to. Of course I couldn't return to bar work or my previous job. Never saw my car again either, which didn't matter since I wasn't going to be driving any time soon. But still, all was not lost – I still have the ring.

GRAFFITO

He shouldn't have taken her there. It was *our* place, the Old Rec. Where we had the first smoke, and the first quarrel – and where we first made love.

I only went down there on my own for a chance to focus on whether I should ask him to move in. It had been hard to make up my mind – I would miss my freedom, but I needed him for myself.

The decision, however, was easier than it might have been. As I turned the corner I saw the familiar black leather jacket slung over our special wall, covering his spray paint on the concrete that once read "I love you". It had now crumbled to "I love" and that hurt.

Then I heard them, my best friend's voice squealing and shouting his name, and his so very familiar groan. I crept away, but gave him what for when he finally turned up. We were no longer an item.

But he came back, asking forgiveness with a hypocritical It's-you-I-love. I said yes. Now he lies silently on my sofa, beads of sweat scattered like diamonds around his once-dear face. I trace a pattern through them with my finger, then pass my hand lightly across his forehead and find it cold. The eyes are open but his expression is blank with just a faint twist of the lips.

Still, he'd enjoyed his last cocktail. I'll miss him, I think.

TONIC

I loved my special tonic.

It invigorated me, inspired my poetry, increased my desire, and he wasn't about to complain about that. My performances were discussed and written about, and the anthologies were selling fast. Life was sweet, and we holidayed in Bali.

"You ought to bottle it. It'd make you a fortune," they said.

Still, every now and then I'd get a bit run down. Then he would lead me gently into the kitchen, take my favourite little lime green knife to his wrist, and hold his hand to my mouth. And off I'd go again.

MAIL

The letterbox snapped shut; two envelopes on the mat.

"Our post gets later every day," Esme grumbled, struggling to get out of her armchair. Joe leaped up.

"Sit down, mother. I fetch the post. You don't."

"It might be for me."

"It won't be."

Joe strode into the hall. The brown envelope addressed to him, marked 'Urgent' in red, he tossed roughly onto the small table, which set petals falling from the dead roses. The white envelope was addressed to Esme, in his sister's handwriting. He stuffed it into his back pocket.

"Just one for me," he said.

Disappointed again, Esme sat back and examined the veins on the back of her hands. Still no word from Elizabeth. Surely the copy of the will must have arrived by now?

COMING TO TERMS

In the four ghastly months since it happened, this was the first time her face had showed real delight.

"Guess what?" she asked him breathlessly.

"Tell me."

"We've had hedgehogs in the back garden. Well, one, at least!"

She dragged him by the elbow to have a look. A small piece of dark, shiny excrement near the pan of water left out for the birds, and he tried hard to look impressed. She assured him it was left by a hedgehog. He wondered how she knew.

An interest in wildlife could be a turning point, Robin thought then. The loss of their four-year old daughter in April had completely devastated her, to a degree beyond Robin's comprehension. Their doctor assured him that eventually she would begin to look outwards at the world once again, but in the meantime their relationship had seemed to be on hold, in more ways than one. Of course he had been absolutely gutted too, and still was – little Chloe had, after all, been their only child. It remained raw, and they rarely mentioned it now, but he had returned to work and she had not.

That evening, from across the room he watched her feverishly trawling the internet and eventually he had to ask.

"Looking up hedgehogs, Jess?"

She tapped a few more keys before looking across at him. "No – trailcams."

"What's a trailcam?"

She beckoned him to look at what she'd found, and explained the trailcam as a movement-activated recorder for capturing wildlife activity within its range. He thought it was expensive, but it would be worth it if it helped her to come to terms. He hoped for another child.

The trailcam arrived three days later while Robin was out, and she tore open the package. The instructions were complex, but she worked her way through them, sorting out the settings one by one until it was done. Subconsciously she wanted this to be totally her own project, and she wandered around the garden deciding where to fix the pole and how to attach the trailcam to scan the area.

Robin was delighted to find that she'd set it all up, and they had a bottle of her favourite Gavi with dinner. They drank to the hedgehog.

The next morning, for the first time in ages, Jess was up first and brought him tea in bed. There was a sparkle in her eyes, and she told him she might start looking out for bats during these late summer evenings. Seeing her like this, he hated himself for constantly hoping for a revival of their sex life, but he couldn't deny it. He put an arm around her.

"Come back to bed for a few minutes? I don't have to leave for an hour."

She froze for a moment, then started to dress. Said she had 'things to do'. He sighed and drank his tea. He promised to look at the memory card from the trailcam with her when he got home.

As soon as he'd gone, Jess dashed out into the garden and retrieved the card. Just as they used to do with the cards from their cameras, looking through holiday and family photos, she slotted it into the side of the television and waited. It flagged up one file. Might it be the phantom hedgehog? More likely one of the neighbourhood cats prowling around searching out any mice or shrews that might be out and about. She opened the file.

The trailcam had indeed captured a fleeting visit of the hedgehog, and she thought about putting some food out for it that night. But, oddly, the garden behind it looked a little misty, as though there was a smudge on the lens. She ran the thirty-second long piece again with the same result, and noted with satisfaction that she'd set the date correctly, August 26th.

Robin was surprised and impressed that she'd viewed the night's recording already; he hadn't especially been interested himself in news about the hedgehog except that it seemed to energise her. It was enough to hear about it from her.

Predictably, the trailcam was to be kept in operation every night, even when it rained. And it did rain. Jess cleaned the lens carefully but three days later there had been no further 'sightings'; Robin wondered aloud whether it was worth keeping going with it. Jess was horrified and he immediately backtracked.

On the evening of the 30th it was raining hard, but the instructions insisted the cam was all-weather.

The next morning Jess's routine - seeing Robin off to work before checking the memory card - continued. Again there was no hedgehog, but then she noticed. There was no rain to be seen on the recording, and the date was wrong – August 20th. This was frustrating. But wait – the misty patch had returned ten seconds into the clip, and seemed to be taking some kind of shape.

Jess shivered. Maybe Robin was right and she was having more difficulty than she'd thought in 'coming to terms'. Surely she wouldn't need outside help? But if she was imagining things which weren't there, well then maybe. She ran the file again, same thing. She took the card from the television and replaced it in the trailcam. For once, at 9.30 in the morning she poured herself a small brandy, and then sat down to check the instructions for setting the date. She was sure it had been right the first time, but best not to mention the glitch until she'd had a chance to sort it out. When she checked the settings, though, they seemed to be correct.

Two nights later, the shape had reappeared. This time Jess was sure it was taking a human shape, though still unclear. She ran it twice more before remembering to check the recorded date: July 20th. She felt dizzy and sick, and refused to let in the thought that was beginning to form in her mind. The shape, the date – this was getting out of hand. She was, as he would say, losing it. She decided to tell him and make him look, leaving the memory card next to the screen.

On his return, Robin was shocked to see the change in Jess. He carried on as normal, but watching from the corner of his eye and waiting to see if she would confide in him. She offered nothing except a robotic preparation of the evening meal, and eventually frustration forced his hand.

"You OK, Jess? You seem a bit, what can I say, on edge."

She hesitated. Was this a good time? Maybe there wouldn't be another opportunity.

"There's something I want you to see from the trailcam. I won't tell you what – I'd like you just to watch and give me your impression."

"Fine, if you've found something interesting."

"I think I have."

They sat together and she held his hand.

"Well, for a start, the date's been set wrong."

"Just watch."

The half-minute piece played again, and Jess gripped his hand more tightly as she watched the shape. He looked puzzled at the strength of her, but kept watching.

"What's to see? The hedgehog never came – but don't let's lose any sleep over it."

For the first time in her life, Jess fainted.

*   *   *   *   *   *

19

She came round to find herself lying on their bed. He was sitting with her, telling her that she would need help for sure, especially now that her physical health was obviously suffering too. He had not seen the shape.

The trailcam showed nothing over the next few days, other than the hedgehog one night and a couple of times the neighbours' tabby cat. She began to doubt herself once more, and realised she had not been eating well enough.

Then it happened again. This time, the file was dated June 20th and the shape was definitely human. It seemed to take a step towards the camera and was beginning to clear. She was most certainly not imagining it now, but she knew that Robin would not see it and did not ask him. She wrote down August 20th, July 20th, June 20th. Chloe had died in that pointless, terrible road accident on April 20th. Would May 20th be next? And what then?

Three nights later, there was more. Jess expected the file to show May 20th, and gave only brief attention when it did. The shape had further cleared, and again took a step towards the lens. She could not believe what she was seeing – and yet, was this what subconsciously she had expected? The little girl looked solemn, and so like Chloe that just a trace of a smile appeared amongst the tears flowing on Jess's face.

That afternoon, Robin came home early. Unable to concentrate on work, he'd fled the office and promised himself that he'd spend more time with Jess, trying to understand what was happening to her and hoping to persuade her to talk again with their doctor. He was surprised to find her asleep on the sofa. Her eyes were puffy and her face streaked, but she had a strange look more peaceful than he had seen for all of those four months. He touched her cheek and she awoke. They looked at one another in silence for a few moments.

In the night, Jess's dreams were untroubled. She was on a beach, in a garden, at a restaurant, in a car, but always with Robin at her side. In the early hours she woke and watched him as he slept. Her arm wrapping around his shoulder alerted him and he turned towards her, opening his eyes and looking at her with his unspoken question. Then she softened in his arms and they made love slowly, tenderly, both willing partners in this tentative move towards restoring their relationship.

*　　　*　　　*　　　*　　　*　　　*
*

Adjusting to the pattern of the trailcam apparitions, Jess expected a delay before the next time, so in the morning she did not hurry to check for a new file. Although she was totally and intensely involved now, and panicking at the thought of what the next recorded date would be and what it would mean, at the same time part of her wanted to know what the progression would bring. She'd started to hope that their love-making might be the start of a healing process for her and for Robin, and did not want anything to derail them.

Later that day, though, she could no longer resist. The new file was dated, yes, April 20th, the catastrophic date that had destroyed her life. She felt acrid vomit rise in her throat and struggled to keep control. But she could not take her eyes off the screen.

The figure had fully cleared now. A little girl holding – what was it? Jess looked closely - a small hedgehog rolled into a ball. The girl looked at the camera, and approached holding the hedgehog in her hands, arms outstretched towards the lens. She smiled and then started to step backwards.

"No!" Jess shouted. "Don't go. Don't leave us. Chloe? Oh, Chloe." But the girl gradually became just a

21

misty shape and slowly disappeared. Jess sat looking at the screen for a moment, and then with a shaking hand she removed the card from the television. "Thank you, Chloe," she whispered.

*   *   *   *   *   *
                    *

Robin was taking leave so that they could be together. His joy was not for the physical aspect of their relationship – which was still erratic – but for the change in Jess. She looked at him in a different way, spoke softly to him, sat with him in the garden in the quiet of twilight. She spent long hours during the day on the bench on the lawn with a book, sometimes in some faraway place but always with a smile for him. And the trailcam was packed away.

During late September she was sick a couple of times, after feeling nauseous for a few days. He didn't pick it up as quickly as she did, but soon afterwards. They hugged one another, and as they pulled apart he asked, in desperate hope,

"Jess, are you sure you're ready?"

"For what?" She hoped she understood him correctly.

"For another child, and ... to talk to our doctor now?"

She looked into his eyes. "Both, I think."

COBWEBS

She'd told him a thousand times that she didn't want a psychologist.

"You may not want one, but you need one," he'd say. Round and round it went, a long-playing record.

Fears can be overcome, it's said, if only the will is there. But was it?

She could date her fear back to when she was thirteen. The front room, cream deep-pile carpet; she wasn't allowed to wear shoes but she could lie on her front, propped up on elbows, enjoying Top of the Pops while the parents scowled and muttered. Adam Faith was snarling, What do you want if you don't want money?

She had on tartan trousers – called them slacks back then – and a loose, man's shirt untucked. Felt a slight tickle on the ribs on the left side, and she'd rubbed it, like you do.

Then, oh a different feeling. What the heck? Parents not looking, she lifted her blouse and saw it. Or what remained of it. A goddam squashed spider, legs still twitching in its death throes.

"This fear is beyond a joke," he told her. "Now it's cobwebs as well. Look at the blasted cobwebs on our ceiling. You make me ashamed of my own home."

"You could always fix them yourself."

"I could. But so could you."

The cobwebs remained, and grew in number.

Trying to understand, he would hold up pictures of spiders, and she would refuse to look. He'd heard of approach therapy, but she was so bad that he couldn't see how anyone could even start to make it work for her. His patience was draining away.

Her mother came round, and twisted her lip as she studied the ceilings around the house. Promised to deal with them for her, with absolutely all of the gleanings stuffed into a polythene bag, knotted and placed in the dustbin. But the thought of her mother even coming close to touching the things made her sweat.

Soon he began to replace the nagging with a spiteful kind of teasing.

"Watch out behind you!"

"What's that, caught in your hair?"

"Nearly time to let your mother come and do the business. You can watch and learn."

She found a picture of a black widow blue-tacked to the headboard of the bed, just above her pillow. It gave her nightmares but she didn't say, just used disposable gloves to peel it off and throw it out of the window to blow away in the street.

Without telling him, she started seeing a psychotherapist. They talked about her childhood, lots of aspects both before and after, and then she talked about the spider. It made her pulse race, but she liked him, felt fairly at ease, and trusted him not to press her too hard, too early.

With time, she began to feel that the fear might become manageable, and when the therapist asked what her goal might be, she told him she'd like to be able to collect a spider in one of those long tube things with a lid and put it in the garden, then watch it run away. The running was as big a threat as the presence of the thing itself.

At first, they touched only briefly on the fear, but played out in commentary the incident that had started it all. She came to accept it as an unlucky event which was over in a second but which was revisiting her now and needed to be put back into the past. After a few sessions, he showed her pictures of tiny spiders, and she traced their shapes briefly with her finger, shuddering at first but becoming more calm.

She told her partner each time that she was seeing a friend, and though he was unsure, he did not query it because she seemed to be more cheerful of late and was no less physical with him than before.

When the therapist was confident of progress, he went with her to a shop selling exotic pets. They looked at the spiders. Her heart pounded but she kept control, and put her palms on the glass. Then he smiled and hugged her quickly, and her heart raced faster still.

After only three more visits, he felt that she should stop the sessions and reinforce the progress they'd made. They looked at one another and there was a pause.

"We could maybe have a drink to celebrate?" he said. "It's OK to take an ex-client out to celebrate a successful course." She wondered if it would be just the once.

She'd started to use a long feather duster to remove the cobwebs, twirling it as she went, and then hitting the tips against the porch wall to clear them. Never when he was home, but eventually he noticed. She was ready for his sarcasm and he didn't disappoint – he could so easily have just said, well done.

She made a couple of visits to the pet shop, looking casually at the rats, scorpions and iguanas and eventually the spiders. In her head she called them arachnids, which sounded more like plants and was easier. On the last visit she discussed them with the sales girl who spoke of them as one might a pet cat.

That evening, she was yawning loudly by nine-thirty, and told her partner she fancied an early night. She lowered her head and looked up at him. Suddenly alert, he agreed readily. So they locked up and went upstairs.

"After you in the bathroom, then," she said, noting the smile and smoothing of the hair as he left the bedroom. He hadn't noticed the box.

He came back, and took off all but his boxers as she took her turn in the bathroom. "Don't be long, darling."

He splashed on the aftershave she used to love, and checked his face and teeth in the mirror before climbing into bed. He congratulated himself on having a partner who still wanted him, a clever girl who'd got over all that crazy stuff about spiders.

As he rolled over onto his left side to face her side of the bed, he felt a sharp pain. He cursed and threw back the duvet to see what had caused it. Then he saw the black widow. He'd squashed it, and the little bastard's legs were trembling as it died. He cursed it and brushed it away from him with his hand.

In seconds he began to sweat, and dizziness made him fall back onto the pillow. The ceiling was dancing, whirling, and then with a groan he fainted and was dead within the minute.

She waited for a short time, then came back, humming and peering round the door. She threw off the duvet, and fetched the trapping tube with the lid to collect the remains of the lifeless spider. After releasing the contents at the end of the garden, she placed the tube neatly in the cupboard, took out her mobile phone, and called the number at the top of her list.

The people of Fordwich held a festival each year on the feast day of St Anselm.

He was their much-loved eleventh-century local saint, once archbishop of nearby Canterbury and now interred in the cathedral. Each year on April 21st the servants at the manor house were granted the day off, as were the labourers; shopkeepers and merchants closed their doors. Even lords and ladies from other manor houses would mingle with the crowd in the market place. And this year, 1263, events had been meticulously planned, for local records suggested that Anselm was canonised exactly one hundred years earlier.

Milo Chaloner had lived in Fordwich all his life, as had his wife, Estrild. At this time they had been married for some ten years, and had been reasonably comfortable together, although there remained silent shadows in the background. Still, like others, they and their three children were looking forward to the next day's festival. There had been another child, but he had died during his first weeks after crying bitterly and often during his brief time. As was usual for little ones, his body, wrapped in its christening gown, had been taken to an ancient oak outside the village. A small tomb had been hollowed out for him within its massive trunk, and Estrild had gently placed him within, watching and weeping as the elders sealed the tomb with pieces of the bark held together by mortar. His remains would feed the tree in the months to come.

Now Estrild was preparing the slaughtered pig, a job she loathed but it was expected of her.

"You're doing the hog roast again this year, Milo?" she asked, without looking up.

"Aye. And the brewer's supplying the ale."

27

"Anyone helping you with the roast? I'd rather not, myself."

"When you say 'anyone' …?"

"I mean Alwyn. He usually helps you."

"Aye, and he helps himself, too. Not only to the meat, neither."

Estrild's knife slipped and cut her hand. He watched as she went to find cloth for a bandage.

On the day itself, the weather was fine. The maypole dances went well, with just the occasional knotting of ribbons, and much ale was bought and drunk. The Greene Man was splendid in his costume of branches, leaves and grasses, and he lit the bonfire as the day wore on. The travelling fortune-teller told Estrild that there had been sadness – of course everyone knew about the baby – but said there was more to come and dismissed her without taking her silver.

Two farm hands helped Milo with the hog roast, but Estrild had no interest. Alwyn had stayed away, and she was sorry. She did not mention him further to Milo.

As evening fell, the villagers formed a group and began, as was traditional, to walk the boundary of the village, laying their hands upon established trees in thanks and reciting prayers to St Anselm around any that held living tombs.

As they approached the Chaloner baby's tree, Estrild held on to Milo's arm as the tears welled up. But his arm was stiff and he did not offer comfort. The prayer was said and the group moved on, but not before the Greene Man had noted some dislodged mortar. There was whispering and later he, with two others, returned to the tree. They studied the mortar carefully, and it was decided that the tomb must be checked.

The replaced bark pieces were removed, and they peered inside. The body of the baby was badly decayed while the gown was in fair form, but doubled up and pressed against it was another that should not have been. A man, not long placed.

"That looks to me like Alwyn," said one of the farm hands.

"It's Alwyn all right," said the other. And so it was.

The news spread quickly back to the group, and they were shocked. Alwyn had been a striking young man who featured in the dreams of many of the local girls, though as far as anyone knew, he had not taken up an offer in the village. There were rumours of a lover, possibly in Canterbury itself, but no proof.

Estrild was grief-stricken once again, and Milo spoke harshly.

"It's months since we lost the child. You've three others to look after, and they need you to be strong. So be strong."

As Estrild made her way tearfully to their bedchamber, she heard Milo muttering but could not make out his words.

"Best thing for the bastard child. Together with his father until the tree be felled."

THE STONES, THE STONES

The great storm of September 1390 in the Bay of Biscay was feared by every seafaring man. Even so, the French wine boats had been commissioned and their men ordered to sail. They would need to stay close to the shore as they navigated northwest and around the French cape to bring their cargo of claret from Bordeaux to Southampton. The shortest route across would be treacherous.

No men were lost, but all hands were watchful as they approached the Isle of Wight, for piracy was rife and in the past they'd had to trade wine for their lives. There was no visible threat, but still they used the sails of their cog and all oars to reach safe waters in the shortest time.

Relaxed and triumphant as at last they drew near to the quay, some of the sailors began to goad the quiet but strong and hardworking Yves Bliaud, causing him to blush.

"Hey, Yves, bet you're hoping that your Matilda Godestone will be there to greet you!"

"Why don't you bring her back to France with us? We'll look after her."

They roared with coarse laughter.

"Yes, then you can make her Madame Matilda Bliaud – she'd soon forget her old man."

As they moored by the sheds, Yves scanned the noisy groups of merchants, taxmen and porters. He saw Matilda at the back of the crowd; their eyes met and she gave a signal. She looked more *charmant* than ever, even with her long blonde hair modestly netted at the back and the dull grey gown showing its age. As the sailors made vulgar gestures to Yves and shouted to Matilda, she rushed away and he was sorry.

By late afternoon, the barrels of wine had been off-loaded, checked, taxed and claimed, then rolled away to the merchants' vaults by sweating porters for a penny apiece. The quayside became quiet, and the sailors repaired to The Red Lion where there would be a keen welcome from the barmaids and other local girls. Not that Yves was interested. He had never been bold with women, but ever since he met Matilda, two trips before, he'd been unable to put her out of his mind. Miraculously she showed feelings for him too, and they had even kissed lightly last time before he lost his nerve.

Yves picked up his second flagon of ale ('filthy stuff to a Frenchman') when the public house door opened and Fulco Godestone strode in. He shot a glance at Yves, who looked away. Fulco's friends and fellow stonemasons beckoned him over.

"How do you fare, Fulco? Is Master Symon Lancaster paying you well for your work?"

Fulco grunted. "No – he owes me for a week's repairs on his vault. He knows it, too; he's still keeping that account of who does what and anything else that goes on. I'd give a king's ransom to be able to read it."

The others laughed, loudly because of the drink. "What, you? Read? No - he knows his written secrets are safe from you!"

Two or three flagons later, Yves had worked up the courage to speak to Fulco.

"How it go, Fulco? I remember you work on a vault."

"Aye. Poor workmanship when it was first built. But it's coming along."

"And your wife? She is Matilda, no?"

The room fell silent. Word gets around.

"Not your affair, Bliaud. You leave her alone."

"I only say because she beautiful. You are lucky man."

Fulco started up from his chair but others held him down. Yves left The Red Lion in haste and headed towards the south corner of French Street. At their last tryst, she had said they could meet there once Fulco had gone drinking, and it was confirmed by her signal. She was waiting, her long hair now flowing freely, which was unusual for a woman on her own, but most beguiling. Hesitantly he put his hand out to her, and she straight away embraced him.

They held one another for a few moments, and then they kissed, first tentatively and then with mounting passion.

But they were not unseen. Fulco, always on his guard where Matilda was concerned, had followed Yves. He ran to them and tore them apart; Matilda shrieked as he pushed her to one side. He fought furiously with Yves. Both were large, strong men but Fulco had the better coordination, being a stonemason, and in moments Yves was on the ground, nose bleeding as he spat out his front teeth.

Fulco dragged his wife home, always in dread of losing her. He was a master craftsman but never a scholar, while Matilda could read, write, cook and sew, and speak of ideas that he did not always understand. He could only hope that she still cared for him; after all, she had lately bought him a silver buckle, etched his initials upon it, and sewn it to the side of his rough surcoat to remind him of her. Not that she was ever far from his thoughts.

Fulco could not sleep, and in the early hours he crept out with a candle and the key to the Lancaster vault. He let himself in, trod carefully down the narrow steps, and picked his way past the new wine barrels to the fireplace. From a heap of square stones ready to repair its back wall, he chose one the size of his fist and placed it in a corner by the steps.

He then went to hunt out Yves in the wine sheds; the sailors often dossed down there to sleep off the ale and be ready to sail at first light. He felt curiously calm.

Then, retching at the stench in the airless shed, he found his quarry.

"Hey, Yves. I wanted to say sorry for hurting you earlier. Still find it hard when other men admire my wife."

Yves was sleepy. He lisped through the gap where his front teeth had been. "That nothing. Forgotten."

"I have something to give you to make up for losing your teeth. It's in the vault. Will you come?"

"Now? No - I need sleep. Sailing in the morning."

"Yes, now. I don't want Lancaster to see it in the morning."

Fulco hurried him to the vault, lit the candle and led the way down the steps.

"Look, Yves, there in the far corner. Don't you think that carving of mine looks like Matilda? I want you to have it."

As Yves strained to see in the gloom, Fulco picked up the stone in the corner and tucked it under his cotte, but Yves heard the grating noise and became suspicious. He spun round, realising he had been tricked. He lunged at Fulco and they fought briefly. Yves, with no weapon, snatched the buckle from Fulco's surcoat and tried to use it to strike the other man's face. But Fulco was quicker. The stone struck Yves so hard on the side of his head that his face jerked to one side as his body buckled and he slumped lifelessly to the floor.

Checking that no-one was around in the street above, Fulco set about removing the stones from the fireplace. The weather was still early-autumn warm, and the brazier would not be needed for Lancaster's wine clients for a month at least. Once the stones were out of the way, he dragged the body into the space, and forced it into its smallest shape before the stiffness would set in. He mixed mortar using water from his leather flask, and used it with the stones to make the false wall that would entomb Yves' body for centuries. It wasn't until he had done his work and returned home that he realised his buckle was missing. He must have lost it in the fight, but it could be retrieved when he returned in the morning.

Matilda had not woken.

Soon after dawn, the sailors were gathering at the quayside to prepare for their journey back to Bordeaux. There were bales of wool and silk to load; they were much easier to handle than the heavy barrels of wine, and the men were soon ready to sail. Then they noticed.

"Hey. Anyone seen Yves Bliaud?"

"Not since last night. Surely he didn't manage to fool Fulco and spend the night with his wife?"

"If he had, he'd be here and anxious to sail out of the port before Fulco found out."

The crew waited for as long as they dared, but eventually the tides and the length of the journey ahead forced them to leave without him.

Meanwhile, Symon Lancaster had heard the gossip at the quay, and could not wait to pull out his lead box of parchments to make a note that a sailor, one Yves Bliaud, had not turned up to sail back to France. This was a rare event, as crews could not easily spare a man. Lancaster expected that Yves was somewhere sleeping off the drink, or he could have deserted and found a cart to take him to another town. He prepared his quill and ink and made reference to the facts under that day's date before locking the parchment away in its box.

At the vault, Fulco had not found his buckle. When he heard footsteps he pretended to be busy smoothing off the mortar in the fireplace as though it had just been applied. Lancaster was impressed with the speed of his work, and made a mental note to pay less than agreed. Thoughtfully he surveyed the rest of the vault, running his hands along the stones in the walls. Looking upwards, he noted with irritation that ashlars in two of the ribs that reached from wall to centre roof were losing their mortar and looking unsteady. He supposed that repairing them would be a necessary insurance. These details would be entered on his parchments.

"Look, Fulco. Your next job is to set these ashlars solid. You'll need more mortar I imagine?"

Fulco was glad. He could make the work take a good week and be paid accordingly. He would commission a new buckle from the same silversmith to match the one he'd lost, and Matilda would never know. He would just say it had come unstitched.

Back at home for a midday meal, he found Matilda setting out bread, cheese and ale in the kitchen, and he sat down. She was unpacking vegetables from her basket, with her back to him.

"I heard down at the quay that one of the sailors went missing and their cog had to sail without him."

"So they say."

"Do you know what had happened to him?"

"When you say 'him', I think you know it was Yves Bliaud."

"I didn't know."

Matilda did not join him at the table, but busied herself around the kitchen until he finished his meal, wiped his sleeve across his mouth, and set off for the vault. He was ready to start on the stone ribs.

Without a glance at the newly bricked fireplace, Fulco rolled one of the barrels over to the rib stones, and climbed upon it to study the state of them, and to judge how much mortar he would need to settle the ashlars firmly back. He put his hands either side of the central stone and gently eased it back and forth. It moved too readily and he was not prepared.

The old, crumbling mortar started to fall, and Fulco was not quick enough. The stone shifted and toppled, knocking him off balance and onto the ground. Those either side followed, leaving him sprawled on his back groaning under their weight, his ribs and legs smashed and the side of his face scraped away. He shouted for help as best he could. Even that was painful, and there was nobody to hear his cries. Soon there were two corpses in the vault.

Symon Lancaster found him the next day, and was not pleased. He hadn't especially liked Fulco but he was a good worker and another would be hard to find at short notice. Added to that, the vault ribs were now in an even worse state, and - worse - he would feel obliged to support Matilda in some way; it would be expected.

Fulco was buried in the local churchyard at his employer's expense, and all was duly noted down on the parchments and sealed away in the lead box to lie unknown and undisturbed under the floor after Lancaster's death.

*   *   *   *   *   *

September 1990

Historian Sarah and Joe from the city council's archaeology department had been asked to make a detailed inspection of the city's vaults as possible tourist attractions, and to talk with the occupants of the merchants' houses above for some background.

Lancaster's vault was first in their sights, and they examined it eagerly, making sketches, scribbling comments, and photographing from all angles. They noted the patching of the ashlars above with stones that did not quite match, and wondered at the limited size of the space in the fireplace – it seemed too shallow to take a brazier or even to store barrels.

In the house above, they knew how to look for undiscovered nooks and corners, places successive owners had not thought to disturb. Under a loose floorboard they found the locked lead box, thick with dust and without any key, but it was a moment's work to force the ancient lock, even with hands trembling with excitement.

Most of the parchment notes were still readable to the trained eye, after all this time and in the elaborate script favoured by their writer. Sarah studied one of the more legible sheets, and read it out as far as she could.

"Septembr 25 yeare of our lorde 1390 Excitement at quay - a sailer, sayd to be one Yves Bliaud, did not return to boate for France. He has not been seyne. Septembr 26 Fulco stonemayson kill'd in my vault today while reparing loose ashlars. Will have to get another man to worke. His wyfe Matilda has little money so I give her worke in my house as cooke and must pay for buryal."

They visited the church, where ancient records showed the burial of Fulco Godestone, husband of Matilda, though any grave markings had long since vanished.

Back at the vault, Joe was thoughtful. "Say, Sarah, d'you think it could be worth looking again at that fireplace? I can't work out a logical explanation for it."

"Well, that might give us the reason for its size, so shall we do it?"

The fireplace was, indeed, excavated with great care, and fragments of a skeleton were revealed. In the same space was a fine silver buckle, etched with 'F G'.

Joe gasped. "Fulco Godestone, I bet! So it looks as though he wasn't buried in the churchyard after all – he's been here all the time."

"But then who's in the churchyard? Could it be the French sailor? And why did Lancaster and the pastor record the grave as Fulco's?"

"It's a mystery all right, Sarah. One to keep the tourists guessing, I'd say."

RIPPLES

She once bit her baby brother, and it had felt so good. The smack from her mother was nothing compared to the satisfaction. The little sod never gave anything back, just take, take her parents' love, all those presents and the cloying attention of strangers. There were other times, but only when no-one would see.

From that day, when she saw a baby there was this urge to damage it and she would have to turn away since it was too late now to get away with it. Of course she grew up certain that there would never be any of her own.

Now she is standing on the jetty, watching the ripples on the lake, and thinking of Mal and his relentless questioning: "Still no sign? Best keep on trying, then!"

Give it time, she'd say softly, digging her fingernails hard into her palm. She loved Mal, she really did, but had never talked to him about It. She wanted their relationship to stay just as it was, yet she sensed that Mal was cooling; he hinted that a baby might bring them closer again (but not that it would bring back his love).

Another boat passes, and as she stares at its undulating wake the churning nausea strikes, then acrid vomit fills her throat. Leaning over the jetty, she throws up into the water. But once again she knows there will be no baby; when the time is right it will join its foetal sibling within the grey-green depths of the lake, leaving just a momentary ripple for a life that never was.

THE GAME

Monday

It was the way he'd looked at her. On the tube that evening, the Piccadilly Line. He appeared at Holborn, one stop after hers, in a black leather coat, a striped scarf wrapped twice around his throat.

Thank God she was looking good. Otherwise, who knows?

She knew what he was thinking of course, and lowered her eyes in sham bashfulness. Always a hook.

Caz was in no hurry. She could take her time with this one, place herself in his path often but not always. He'd be sure to notice any absences, which always added to the intrigue.

He left the train at Turnpike Lane, one stop before hers at Wood Green.

Tuesday

Good timing, as ever, for the train home. Approaching the stop before his, she made a big deal of buttoning her coat and getting ready to leave the train. She glanced briefly over her shoulder before stepping onto the platform. Yes, he was watching, perhaps surprised. And yes, it meant an extra walk for her, but it was necessary. Then eye contact until the carriage was past. This was going well.

Wednesday

Same time, and she lifted her brow as she met his gaze. He hesitated, then came to sit beside her.

"Hi."

Eyes cast towards his waist, she nodded just once.

"Seen you around. I'm Daniel."

"Caz."

She began to shred the tissue in her left coat pocket. Always the left side. Nothing further was said, though she felt his nearness acutely. Let him think there was no great interest as yet.

Thursday

Same train home, but packed that evening. She was sandwiched between two women and he had to stand, but they exchanged a glance. So sweet. He left the train at her stop, right behind her, his hand gently against her back. Not unexpected at this stage, and she looked at him with a question in her eyes.

In fifteen minutes, she was sitting straight-backed in a coffee shop as he returned to the table with drinks. Black for her (not her usual way) and white with sugar for himself. As he stirred, she saw there was no ring – not that it told you much these days. They swapped details of jobs, their ages, where they lived.

"My flat's on Carnaby Road," he told her. "Not Carnaby Street, though, sadly," he laughed, and he watched her face.

"I know where that is."

Now he was fiddling with a button on his jacket. "Sorry if I seemed to be staring. It's just that, well, you reminded me of someone. Sorry."

"No need to apologise. People sometimes tell me that, and anyway, I know the feeling."

Then she started to talk about Rob. Well, the first part. A short, intense relationship that had left her shaken when he decided to go. It was such a shame … She didn't finish the story, didn't say how the rejection was too much to bear.

"Look, Caz, you don't need to tell me if you'd rather not. It's sort of private – isn't it?"

"No, I want to. I want to explain why it happened. I mean, he was young, ambitious."

Daniel held up his hand for her to stop, and she bit her lip and fell silent.

Friday

She went to work very early, so as to get away in good time. Then, making her way to the road, she looked around for a place to keep watch. The park bench would have to do, and with her hat pulled down low over her eyes she would not be recognised.

At the time to be expected, Daniel came striding in her direction on the other side. He looked pensive, which was quite attractive, no doubt thinking about her and wondering why she hadn't been on the train. She looked down as he passed, then watched him enter the block of flats just beyond the second lamppost from her bench. She pulled out her notebook and pen, and wrote 'Carnaby Court', then replaced the rubber band around it and pushed it into her bag.

Once he was out of sight, she strolled over to the block. A quick look at the column of doorbells listed Daniel Fairway in flat 3. Fairway.

Monday

They chatted lightly on the way home, standing side by side and close this time, and she talked about the novel she'd begun to write, a thriller. But by the time they parted, he still hadn't suggested meeting again socially. This was a glitch, hopefully temporary; they should be further forward by now, though she felt sure that he wanted to ask her. It took only four days with Rob – but then he'd been younger and always so confident.

"See you tomorrow?" he asked.

"For sure."

But on the Tuesday, Daniel was not where he was supposed to be.

Wednesday

She left work early again, pulled on the hat, and made her way over. Taking up her place on the bench, she was prepared to wait but was absently shredding a new tissue in her left pocket.

She thought about the older man on the train that day; not the first time she'd seen him. He'd shown a definite interest, and he looked quite good for his age – she guessed fifty-five - but he'd have to wait for a while. Two or three weeks, maybe, she should be ready round about then.

Daniel walked towards his block, no scarf and on her side of the road this time. He was surely a looker, one you wouldn't pass up. He glanced at her, and there was hesitation. Big mistake of hers, making eye contact. He turned to face her fully.

"Caz?"

No point in denying it now.

"What are you doing here?"

She thought quickly. Told him that she knew someone in the road but not which house. Then she shook her head and twisted her fingers together in a mock nervousness.

"Sorry. I'm lying. I wanted to tell you my hours have changed, so we may not meet up like we usually do."

He looked surprised. "Good of you, Caz, thanks, but not necessary. Although I confess, I did wonder. And if you don't mind my asking, …"

Caz held up her right palm. "It's OK. Not to worry. Doesn't matter." She walked away. He still hadn't asked for another meeting; this was not going well, some adjustments would have to be made.

Thursday

She wrote him a letter, first class, in brown ink using a fountain pen and neat script. A dark stain remained on the middle finger of her left hand. The colour of old blood.

'Hi, Daniel. Hope you don't mind me writing – and asking – but I wondered if we could meet up like we did before. Only this time, maybe a drink? My treat – I've been such an idiot. Please call me. Love, Caz xx' Forgot to include her number – uncharacteristic.

Monday

He didn't see her, although she'd been watching as he scanned all around on the train, at the station, along his road. His shoulders looked tense – must be upset, thinking he wouldn't see her again. It was easy enough to find his landline number, and he jumped when his phone rang late at night. It quickly stopped. 1471 – "The caller withheld their number." After a few minutes she called again.

"Hi. It's Caz."

"Oh, hello, Caz. Haven't seen you for a bit. What've you been up to?"

"Did you get my letter?" After a few moments, "Just wanted to say sorry again, and hope I've not upset you. I wondered if you meant to get back in touch, but then I realised I hadn't given you my mobile number." She recited it slowly, for him to write down.

He spoke quickly. "Actually, I'd like to. Very much. Just that I've had a lot to think about. If you can give me a day or two, I'll get back to you. Take you up on your offer."

"Is it because I still remind you?"

"That's what first caught my interest. But I hope we can get past that."

"So do I. And don't leave it too long. I miss our chats."

Wednesday

Another letter written. Daniel, are you still around? Haven't seen or heard from you. Please can we meet? I really need to see you. There's something I'd like to run past you. In case you might have misheard my mobile number, here it is again.

Caz had been wondering why this one wasn't straightforward. Rob had been easier at first, but he made a mistake cooling and then turning her down for a better offer. And look what happened – all his fault. He wouldn't be playing that card again. And now, she so hoped that Daniel would be different, and there was still a good chance that he might be.

Friday

The silence was becoming frustrating, infuriating. But that evening her phone buzzed. A text from Daniel. Sorry for delay. Meet Black Dog tomorrow 8pm? Your round.

He deserved to wait for her reply.

Saturday morning

Hi D. That wd be good. But 1st date – shd be your round.

Now we're getting somewhere.

Saturday evening

He was there when she arrived at 8.10. He brought back the drinks – large scotch with water, and one Campari and soda. She disliked Campari but knew he would think it chic. She quizzed him about his recent absence, but he shifted in his chair and gave a vague change-of-routine explanation. He asked what she wanted to run past him, and it took her a moment to recall what she'd said. She hedged, then said it was just the plot for her novel. Wouldn't be wise to go too fast.

After a second drink, they left – her suggestion, to go for a walk. Conversation was easy and relaxed but nothing of importance. They parted later on the train, and she – seeming impulsive – leaned across and kissed him lightly on the cheek, at the same time brushing her hand gently down the side of his face. He could call her after the weekend.

Monday
No sign on the train, but the older man was there, now looking intently at her for sure.

Wednesday evening
Her mobile rang, flagging up Daniel. This was good.

"Hi, Daniel. Good to hear from you."

He cut her short. "Look, Caz, I'm really sorry I didn't call, but something's come up. I need to explain."

"I'm listening."

"There's no easy way to say this."

"Just spit it out."

"The firm want me to move to Manchester soon, and I …"

"*What?*"

"Manchester. There's a new hub there, and we had a meeting. I've just told them I'll go."

A short silence, then, "Why?"

"It's the career break of my dreams. I can't turn it down. You must see that?"

"When will you go?"

"Three weeks. Caz, I'm really sorry. We were getting on well, weren't we? We can meet for a drink again to talk about it, say tomorrow, if you'd like to – same time, same place?"

"All right."

Oh Daniel. This was not going to end here.

Thursday

She was first at The Black Dog this time, 7.45, to be sure of a good, quiet table. In the circumstances he could buy the first drink again.

By 8.10 he hadn't arrived, and she rechecked her notebook before replacing the rubber band. She shredded another tissue in her left pocket. Then he came.

"Sorry, sorry. Worked late, but here now. What'll you have?"

The bar was becoming busy, and noisy with a quiz night. She hadn't planned for that. Buying the round took several minutes, but he returned with the same drinks as before.

He looked nervous, as well he might. "You look great, Caz. Purple really suits you."

She pretended not to hear above the noise.

"I said, you look great."

"Thanks. So do you, Daniel." And she realised it was true. Could this really be going to end, almost before it had begun?

He asked politely about her novel. She let him persuade her to tell him, and described it as a murder mystery.

"Wow! Not written from experience I hope."

She dropped her glass and the pink campari spread across between them. He fetched a cloth from the bar and started to mop the table, taking care to stop the liquid from splashing onto her frock. His hand brushed against hers, and she shivered and stared at him.

"I'll get you another."

She refused, complained about the heat and the noise, and, picking up her clutch bag, suggested they might go outside to the car park to cool down. He agreed, picked up his drink and guided her through the crowd that was growing around the bar. They leant against the low wall of the car park and he asked again about Rob.

A few more sketchy details. She'd liked Rob a lot, but he told her out of the blue that he'd met someone younger and that their relationship was over.

"What did you do?"

"What anyone would have done." She looked steadily into his eyes.

"Most people would have been down for a bit, but then would have tried to move on."

"Not me."

He looked at her sharply, and waited. She put her right hand behind her back, still holding the bag.

"Look, Daniel. I wasn't sure about you at first, but now, well I think I might be falling for you. I *really* don't want you to call it a day and move up to Manchester. Surely it's not too late to change your mind? *Please?*"

Daniel told her that he liked her very much, and any other time things would have developed, maybe into a lasting relationship. But he had accepted the offer of promotion and would not go back on his word. After all, they could still meet up at weekends, and call one another.

He noticed the tears in her eyes, the clenched fist, but not the knife in her left hand behind her.

"I didn't think I could ever love, not like this. I realise it was wrong last time, not really love, and there was a need to punish. But this is different. Daniel, I'm not able to be without you. Could I at least come with you?"

"Caz, please. Calm down. We were supposed to be talking this through." His pulse was racing. There was no-one else around. He held his hands towards her in a gesture of despair.

Her eyes were wide as she brought the knife around and pointed it towards him.

He dropped his glass and it shattered at their feet. "Put that down, Caz. Drop it. You're in a state. You can't mean this – you love me, remember? And you shouldn't hurt the one you love."

"You did."

She thrust the knife towards him, but he grasped her wrist and pushed it hard downwards and away from him to make her let go. As she struggled, he needed more force. But too much. The knife slid low into her abdomen, surprisingly making no sound. She doubled up in pain, puzzled eyes looking up at him.

"Oh my god. Caz!"

She sank slowly onto the cold concrete. After a few stunned moments, he turned away and threw up. Then he placed his folded jacket under her head, knelt beside her, and clasped her hand. She was looking towards him, now in shock, colour leaving her face and blood flowing across the purple fabric of her frock and pooling at her side.

"Daniel", she gasped. "For the first time in my life, I really, really loved someone."

"I know," whispered Daniel. But she would not hear.

LEAVING

James had sworn his love, and he was good to me for quite some while. I'd never seen him as a long-term proposition, but even so it was an insult and an inconvenience when he later met someone else and left - he should never have done that.

I then became quite fond of his mate Joe, but his parents took a dislike to me for no reason. In the end they proved too powerful for him so he gave in and dumped me. He should never have done that.

More recently it seemed that good old Tom was besotted with me. I wasn't quite so keen at first – although he's a likeable enough chap - but we made love and he moved in. Over time things became very comfortable between us, and quite fun too. Then – why does this keep happening? – he seemed to withdraw. Little things at first: went out with the lads just a little more, bought me tights for my birthday, and fondant chocolates that he'd know were not my favourites. Soon after that he told me that his work would soon be taking him abroad. Something had to be done.

Expecting him home, I took the beautiful solid silver stiletto from the drawer where it nestled among my silk underwear and ran my finger along the blade. Making plans to leave me? He should never have done that.

UGLY DUCKLING

Costain was at his desk in the early evening, trawling the records for any link to a young man in a cell downstairs. Just as he took another bite from the cheese roll, his phone rang for the umpteenth time that day. He carried on chewing – nothing would keep him from his food.

"Yes, Black. What've you got?"

The sergeant sounded breathless. Always a sign of trouble.

"Sir, just had a call on my mobile from the hospital. A crash victim died on the ward."

"Get away. And what's it got to do with us? Anything special?"

"Yes guv. They thought he wasn't too bad when he was admitted, but now they've found him dead in the bed with some unusual marks and the bedding all over the shop."

Costain sighed. It had been a long day and he wouldn't be home any time soon. "OK, sergeant. Meet you there in twenty."

They arrived at the hospital at the same time and headed up to Ward D6 nurses' station.

"I'm DI Costain and this is Sergeant Black. You have some suspicions about a death on the ward?"

The ward sister, tall, lean and serious, pulled out some notes and led them to a small side ward with just one bed. As she opened the door, a number of machines could be seen – a drip, heart rate and pulse monitor, the usual. In the bed was the body, now separated from all the tubes and clips and with the eyes staring. The bedclothes were crumpled and partly pushed to one side.

"We haven't touched anything, of course. Normally we would have tidied up, especially as the family will be here in less than an hour, but since we were unsure …"

"Yes, fine, sister. Now could you just tell us what you know?"

The victim, Paul Malone, had been in a car crash. There were no apparent internal injuries, and he hadn't seemed too bad and was coherent on admission, still arrangements had been made for scans just to be sure. When the nurse came to prepare him, she found what they all now saw.

Costain approached the bed and studied the position of the sheet and blanket intently. He thought it was consistent with a struggle. Then he began to look carefully at discolouration starting around Malone's face and neck, and noticed the blood vessels in the eyes. He peered at a small grey-brown feather at the edge of the pillow. "Any reason why you don't use foam pillows, sister? I'd have thought they'd be more hygienic."

"Oh we do. Use foam, I mean. So many people are allergic to down these days."

"And it's cheaper?"

"Well yes, that too."

Costain glanced at DS Black and nodded towards the pillow, so the sergeant scooped the feather into a tiny evidence bag and sealed it. Costain asked to see the doctor who'd certified the death.

While they waited for the Scene of Crime officer, the photographer and the doctor, the sister read out what they knew of Malone's background. At admission he'd told them that he was head of science at the local academy – or 'comp' as Costain would still call it - and he was aged 38. No stated religion. Unmarried, living in a flat, parents living on the south coast but now on their way to ID the victim. No earlier hospital records.

"Was he in this ward on his own, right from admission?"

"Yes, Inspector. We had the space and he was still in a state of shock."

"Any visitors at all yet?"

"Not as far as we know. As yet we've told only you and the parents."

"Any info on the car crash?"

"The paramedics were called by another motorist who arrived after the accident. The car was a write-off but there doesn't seem to have been anyone else involved. Apparently there may have been some kind of mechanical failure while he was driving round a bend, and he hit a tree full on."

They thanked the sister, and suggested she could now carry on with her duties. They would stay with the body.

"What do you think, guv?"

"Decidedly suss. I'm no doctor but I'm guessing he's been suffocated. Let's hope the medics can confirm one way or the other."

"If it's murder, then it's a mystery since no-one except the hospital staff, the motorist who reported it, and the parents know he's here, and he certainly wasn't expected." Black took out his pocket book and started making notes.

Costain felt the need for something further to eat; he thought more clearly on a full gut. Leaving his sergeant to mind the scene, he went in search of a snack vending machine. Looked as if it would have to be a prepacked cheese sandwich; he made a mental note to have his cholesterol checked, but probably not before the next scheduled medical, when they would also comment on his weight and his blood pressure. If he could dodge the police medicals, for a while at least, he would.

He sat on a plastic bench to eat, idly wondering whether they'd do a check for him on the quiet while he was there in the hospital. Then his phone rang.

"Guv, the doctor's here. Can you come up?"

The doctor seemed young and very confident. He'd certified the death, for which he'd receive a very welcome fee, and he found it hard to assume a suitably serious expression.

"It seems clear to me that Mr Malone has not died of natural causes," he pronounced.

"And?" asked Costain impatiently.

"And, Inspector, I believe he may have been suffocated. Despite putting up some resistance." He nodded towards the heap of bedclothes.

"*Believe?*"

"All right, he *was* suffocated. Probably with the pillow you see over there on the chair. And note the petechiae around the face." Costain didn't recognise the term but could guess. He wouldn't give the doctor the satisfaction of asking.

*　　　*　　　*　　　*　　　*　　　*

After the photographer had gone, and SoCO too, Costain and Black waited for Malone's parents to arrive. Once the doctor had explained the situation to them – hopefully with at least a little compassion – they could be asked for some background. Friends, enemies, worries, anything that would shed some light on this inexplicable murder.

Frustratingly, the Malones could offer little that was relevant. Paul had been a bit of a loner, they offered, heavily into science and books from an early age. They didn't know of any particular friends – or enemies – although his mother thought he'd sounded fairly cheerful on the phone recently and she had been hoping that he had maybe 'met someone'. They hadn't seen Paul for a few weeks, but he had a nice flat and they knew he enjoyed his work and hoped one day to apply for deputy head. That wasn't going to happen now, and the mother broke down completely so that the discussion had to be halted.

Costain and Black were sitting in the Friends of the Hospital café, nursing their teas.

"Thoughts, sergeant?"

"Well, guv, given the fact that Malone was murdered in the hospital after an apparently accidental write-off, it suggests the killer was either a psycho already in the hospital who picked him at random, or else the accident and the murder were linked in some way. Do you think?"

"I do think. I like your second scenario better."

"I'll get hold of the accident report as soon as it's done."

"You need to track down Mr X, the reporting motorist, and any other witnesses who might confirm that Mr X wasn't on the scene *at the time*. And get round to Malone's place to see what you can find out about his movements, visitors, routine and so on. Tonight would be good – unless you've an arrangement to meet any tidy WPCs after work?"

"Huh. Take it you mean Adams? Well, chance would be a fine thing."

"Chop chop, then."

*   *   *   *   *   *

At the block of flats, it turned out that the chap next door had a key to Malone's place, and he showed the DS around. Malone had been a quiet one, very few visitors and no family locally. His car had been his pride and joy, always washing, polishing, admiring.

"Now I come to think of it, though, there was a young man used to call for him occasionally, and they'd go off in Malone's car. Don't know why he didn't come up."

"Can you describe the young man?"

"Maybe mid-twenties, sort of tidy looking I guess. They used to disappear for ages, not that I was particularly watching. White, quite tall, fair hair – nothing else that I noticed. Sorry."

Next morning, Black was at his desk early. As he'd hoped, there was a note with the preliminary findings relating to the vehicle. He puffed out his cheeks; this was good stuff. While checking his notes from last evening's visit to Malone's flat, he listened out for the sound of Costain trudging up the stairs, to be followed by some gasping as he reached the landing. He didn't have long to wait.

"Morning guv. Got some news for you."

"Good grief, man. Give me a chance to get my breath back."

Black explained first what was in the vehicle report. *Slow leak – cause deliberate – in the hose leading to the power steering.*

"Well that's novel, anyway. Makes a change from the old 'brake pipe' trick. And it means it's unlikely to be anyone hospital-based. In which case someone from outside slipped into the ward and finished the business. Did we get the CCTV?"

"I'm going in to the hospital to look at it this morning, guv. And just a thought – probability is that the hose leak thing is down to a male. And that's not being sexist."

Costain smiled; he considered his sergeant to be non-sexist, non-racist, in fact non-everything-bad. Having him on the team was a bit of luck, though it could be frustrating when he stuck rigidly to being 'correct'.

"Track down Mr X yet?"

"Got a rookie onto it, guv. And he'll look for any witnesses – though if Mr X had done the fixing, he wouldn't have wanted to call emergency services or to be involved on the scene at all."

Costain looked thoughtful. "Unless he needed to make sure the job was done. And if it wasn't, he could've got over to the hospital himself."

At the hospital, security located the CCTV for the area around the ward. At around the time in question, they could see a hooded figure in a hurry going towards it, and ten minutes later, leaving. Couldn't tell whether male or female, which was a real pain. Couldn't see the face, no matter how much the image was enlarged, but Black took it with him to the station anyway.

Later, forensics came back about the feather on the pillow – oddly, a duckling feather but no prints of course – and from the crashed car hose, again no clues.

Costain and Black were in the canteen for lunch.

"Well, sergeant, what've we got? Where to next?"

Black frowned. "We have to trace Malone's companion. Relationship could be sexual, brother, work colleague, student, or just a friend."

"Quite so. Look, I want you to check out Malone's recent history – his work, his interests, his hobbies, his social circle. Have another look around the flat. And let's borrow a plod to check street CCTV for the visitor at the flat and maybe have another good look at the mystery figure in the hospital. We could get lucky – they could be one and the same, then we're halfway there."

As Black left to check for any available PCs, Costain called back, "Why not ask for Adams? That could be your way in!"

PC Joanne Adams had not long been at the station. She'd been a successful PCSO in another force, and had gained her Police Law and Community Certificate with ease, so she'd made PC there. Applying to move to Costain's force, she'd surprised him with her in-depth knowledge of the law, calmness and willingness to jump into any difficult situation. He couldn't help thinking that she and Sergeant Black would make a great partnership. Both types.

Adams patiently studied the footage from the street outside the flat, and eventually found what she was looking for. A young man visiting Malone's flat. Nothing obviously suspicious; he didn't appear to be trying to hide his identity – just rang the bell and waited for Malone to show – but his face wasn't clear enough, even with zoom. Then they drove off in Malone's car, parked on the road a couple of doors down. She compared the visitor with the hospital footage and pronounced the two figures to be possibly the same person before returning the tape to the sergeant.

Black didn't want to waste an opportunity, but thought, steady as it goes.

"Fancy a coffee, Joanne? My treat for your efforts?"

"An offer I can't refuse, sergeant."

"It's Kevin. Write it in your notebook."

In the canteen – or 'staff restaurant' – they chatted briefly about the tape, until Black asked her how she came to be in the force. The gossip was that she'd moved across from being a PCSO and then PC on another patch because there were limited opportunities for promotion there.

"Oh, a number of jobs before this. Waitress in a café at first, just something to tide me over. Then temping and eventually in a school."

"A teacher? Which school?"

"You wouldn't know it. Out in East Anglia. And not a teacher, just a lowly assistant."

"Sounds as though you've settled for second best a number of times, Joanne. Do you have ambitions here? The guv says you did very well before."

"How would he know?"

Black chuckled. "He just does. So, are you looking for sergeant's stripes here?"

"You bet. At least, I shall be in a while. In the meantime, ready and waiting for something big to work on. But enough - let's talk about you."

*   *   *   *   *   *

Malone's murder remained a mystery for now, but there were a couple of leads. First, the duckling feather from the dead man's pillow - plenty around, so not much help, but still interesting. It shouldn't have been there; must have been placed, and this troubled Kevin Black. It reminded him of something, and eventually he remembered a similar thing happening three years or so ago. In fact the only unsolved killing in their area. Details on his computer showed that a chief librarian had gone missing and was eventually found in the vaults, the life squeezed out of him between two of those tall metal storage systems where a wheel turned to open or close the gap between any two given sets of shelves. Near to the horribly disfigured body a feather had been found, obviously pushed into the gap after the librarian had died. A duck feather, they said. Couldn't be a coincidence, that. And some of the staff had been so upset that they'd left without another job lined up. Tragic in itself, and to think that the murderer remained free to kill again.

Meanwhile, Paul Malone's neighbour had been in touch. He had seen the young man arriving at the flats just after Black had left – obviously hadn't heard the news. From his front window, the neighbour took a picture on his mobile and, at Black's request, had emailed it to him.

Costain and Black were talking about the link to the previous crime and the young man's picture.

"Do we know who he is, Kevin?"

"Yes, guv. One of the PCs recognised him – he's out of work but he volunteers at the local youth centre and the PC knows him. Says he's all right."

"So. Let's get out that CCTV from the hospital and have a proper look. What did you get from it yourself?"

"Actually I didn't have much of a look. I left Adams to watch it, and she thought the hoodie was probably the same person as the visitor to the flat. I'll fetch the tape."

They both studied the figure heading towards the ward. Costain twitched.

"Hold it just there. Did you see who just walked by, studying some notes?"

Black backtracked a little. "Looks like the sister we spoke to."

"Exactly. And do you remember how tall she was?"

Black thought back. "Ah yes. Well taller than you, guv."

"And how does she match up to the intruder as they pass?"

"I see what you mean. She's a good six to eight inches taller." The penny dropped. "And that mate of Malone's would at least match her for height."

"Quite. Which would seem to let the mate off the hook, don't you think? Perhaps Adams needs glasses."

Kevin was embarrassed for not having checked. "She was only doing what I asked, and in a hurry. But it means we're back to square one."

It seemed that the motive for the killing was still the key, which was a difficult one because Malone sounded like a quiet chap who got on well with the other staff at the school and was well liked by the pupils. Costain wanted to know if every member of staff had been questioned about their relationship with their head of science, especially those in that department. They had, and nothing special had come up. He wondered if anyone had asked the science students if they had anything they could add, but only a general invitation had been given out for them to contact Black if they knew of anything unusual, and nothing had come of it.

Costain asked whether any staff from the school had left shortly before or after the murder, and wanted the same check for the library where the previous 'feather murder' had taken place. He wanted Black to do the checking himself rather than delegate it. Library staff couldn't remember much that hadn't already been said, but one of the assistants recalled someone leaving under a bit of a cloud after a row with the head librarian. There were no available records of who that was, or the reason why he or she left.

At Malone's school it seemed there was competition among the technicians for promotion. They generally started at Level 1, then took exams in the hope of rising to Level 2 and then senior status. One of the longer-serving technicians remembered that a Level 2 chap had been accused of stealing petty cash and had been sacked.

*   *   *   *   *   *

Black was still keen to get close to Joanne, both mentally and physically, and invited her out for a drink. He wanted to talk about the latest case and to see if she had any ideas. She was becoming known as the PC with insight, as well as being a looker.

"Any special reason, sergeant? Kevin, I mean?"

"Yes, there is. I fancied a drink and couldn't think of anyone better to take to the pub."

"Flatterer."

It didn't take long to get started on talking shop. Joanne knew the feathers were significant, and felt they might indicate that the murderer was challenging the police. There could be someone else in the force who would pick up the meaning. Possibly a farm connection - or it could be that his name had a bird connotation.

Kevin laughed. "That'd be that Mr Bird, then." Joanne smiled. She knew he was impressed.

"Look, Kevin. I really want to get involved with the case if you'll let me. I'm more than ready to tackle something like this. What do you think?"

"OK by me. I'll run it past the guv tomorrow."

Costain agreed that Adams could be involved – well she already was, with her work on the tapes. She was invited to sit in on the conversation about the case.

"Anything new, sergeant?"

"Yep – no go on Mr X the 'other motorist' I'm afraid. One, the plod – sorry Joanne, the PC – found a couple of witnesses who said there was no other car on the scene for a several minutes – they didn't have phones on them and had run across to see if they could help. And two, the other motorist was actually *Ms* X."

"Doesn't rule her out."

"Well three, she was a lady in her seventies who had taken the wrong road and was lost. Her family had given her a mobile because it wasn't the first time …"

Joanne interrupted. "So, assuming Malone's neighbour is clear, the only reasonable suspect we have so far, then, is the hooded chap in the hospital who could be the friend at the flat. Is there anything further on him?"

"Him?" queried Costain. "And by the way, they aren't one and the same. Height difference."

The meeting as such broke up, and Joanne left the room feeling wounded. Now Costain had another job for his sergeant.

"Kev, I don't know how you'll take this, but when it was clear that Adams had made a mistake by describing both figures as of the same height, - pretty elementary error - I called the DI at her previous station to see if anything had been unsaid in his reference."

Black looked stunned. He couldn't think what this was about.

"Seems she was after fast tracking to DS and, well, made one or two mistakes in her investigations. Check out where she's been before joining the force, and anything interesting in her history."

*　　　*　　　*　　　*　　　*　　　*

Black's enquiries left him sick. Adams had in the past worked at a library. *That* library. And further, the school where she'd worked in the science department was not, as she'd said, in East Anglia, but local. The member sacked for theft was not reported to the police, but the general opinion was that as a Level 2 technician he was a good worker and always reliable – no-one could believe he'd been guilty of theft. He'd been replaced by an outside applicant.

At the very least, Joanne had lied about her past. Still, desperate to give her the benefit of the doubt, he waited his moment and invited her out to an Italian restaurant. He would carefully try to uncover her history, and he hoped he might tempt her back to the flat afterwards. In his scenario, she would clear up his doubts and then slide into his bed.

In the restaurant, the conversation was general and largely about Black as she asked him about his own past, family, jobs and so on. But she agreed to return to his flat.

Black downed several whiskies while Joanne drank more slowly. Eventually he told her what he knew about her history at the library and in the school. She appeared shocked but was not, in fact, surprised, knowing that most things could not be kept under wraps for ever. As Black began to slur his words, she told him that the head librarian had turned down her application as his assistant, since the previous one had inexplicably left. He deserved what he got.

She added that she had applied for Level 2 at the school after the science technician was sacked for theft, and no, he wasn't guilty. Malone had turned down her application and appointed an outsider, which was his mistake. As Black had once said, she had previously settled for second best, and she'd had enough of being the ugly duckling. She wanted to be a swan, and she would be.

Black's head was swimming. "So, the duckling feathers were yours?"

Joanne lifted her chin and smiled.

"But Malone's car. Power steering. You?"

"You forget, Kevin. I worked at a library. I went back for the information – 629.2872, Technology and Transport."

He wouldn't believe what he was hearing; it made sense but he desperately wished it was all a bizarre joke. Or maybe he was dreaming.

But this was not a dream, as he realised at the last moment when Joanne fetched a knife from his kitchen and plunged it into his chest while holding a feather to his face. He looked at her briefly as his glass fell to the floor, then his eyes rolled and he was gone.

Joanne carefully washed and dried her glass and wiped any possible fingerprint areas including the knife but not the door handle since clearly she had come in. She placed the feather across Black's chest, then took out her mobile and called Costain.

"Joanne. What's up?"

Joanne made small choking noises. "Guv. I'm at Kevin's flat – he asked me to call round, had something to tell me. The door was open, so I …. Please come now. Kevin's dead. Stabbed."

Costain arrived with a PC. What he saw shocked him, even though he'd seen worse many times. His own sergeant. He told the PC to arrest Joanne but couldn't himself look her in the face.

"But guv – I was first on the scene – I called it in – I didn't do it."

"Save it, Adams. I told Black to check you out. He left me his report and I was coming after you anyway. I'm just gutted that I didn't get to you in time."

"You'll regret it, guv. I'm innocent."

"No. You're the ugly duckling and always will be. You'll never turn into that swan."

SANDCASTLE

They left their sandals where the shingle turned to sand.

"Race you to the water."

"I won't race. You always win."

"That's 'cause I'm bigger and better than you."

The mother called to them to stop bickering. Then her suggestion: "Why not make a nice sandcastle, with a deep moat to keep the tide from washing it away?"

They were going to do that, anyway, but didn't say. If she thought it was her idea, then she might get them an ice cream.

The buckets made good, firm towers for the sandcastle, and the girl made a sand soldier to stand guard on the ramparts with a small, sharp piece of flint she'd found for his shield.

But now the sea was closing in. Desperation took hold as they frantically scooped sand from the moat to contain the foaming edges of the waves.

"Come *on*. Dig quicker or we're done for."

Then the one big wave they were dreading crashed onto the beach and sucked back part of the castle – but the guard was left unharmed.

The girl started to whimper, which always annoyed him. In frustration at losing the battle with the sea, and to punish her, he gave her guard on the rampart a mighty kick, sending the broken sand body scattering into the sea. And along with the guard went the sharp flint shield.

Blood stained the sand for a brief moment before being washed away. The girl fell silent and the boy cried. From the pain and because there'd be no ice cream now.

BOTTLES AND POTS

The first three years of their marriage went well. They had so much in common, got on well with one another's extended family, and shared a wry sense of humour.

Any issues were discussed and – usually – resolved. For instance, Charlotte's passion for collecting early Moorcroft pots went a bit far, but they had afforded a large, three-storey Victorian house and David persuaded her to keep her ceramics in one of the small rooms on the top floor. They'd be an investment, at least, and he could keep well clear of them. Then there was his hobby, collecting expensive French red wine – bought by the case, and wheeled out only for special occasions, and then only the one bottle at a time. The cellar was a good place to store it, out of sight and always cool and still. He thought the cobwebs added to the atmosphere, but she thought it rather spooky, especially in such an old house.

The first shaft of doubt struck him one evening. Charlotte was on her way upstairs for a bath, and out of the corner of his eye he saw her pick up her mobile phone from the hall table as she headed up. Why would she need it in the bath?

"You OK, Charl?"

"Yes. Why wouldn't I be?"

"No reason."

David started watching a DVD while she ran the bath, and waited until a couple of minutes after the taps went quiet. Then he left the film to run, and trod lightly up the stairs to listen at the bathroom door.

Her phone conversation was not clear, and he could make out only part of it. She seemed to be speaking in a low voice. He heard 'Saturday' – what were they doing this Saturday? Nothing that he could recall. Then all went quiet except for occasional swirling of the water. He returned to the DVD, poured a whisky and waited.

Charlotte came down in her white towelling dressing gown, and even with her hair damp and hanging limply, he thought how gorgeous she looked. She kissed the top of his head as she went to sit opposite him, and he poured her a drink. He wished she could be more discerning with wine, but a cheap Chardonnay was her choice. As her dressing gown parted to reveal a slim thigh, he felt a stirring of desire.

They both watched the film for a while, but after a couple of drinks he thought it safe to sound her out.

"How'd you like to go out for the day at the weekend, Charl? We haven't had a free day for a while, and it would be great to have lunch out and, maybe, a walk down by the river in the afternoon. Buy you a cream tea, too, if you like. Say, Saturday?"

She glanced at him briefly. "That would be lovely, Dave – oh, but I've just remembered. I promised Bella that I'd go with her to shop for a going-away outfit for her wedding." Bella was soon to marry David's brother.

"Can't you do that on Sunday? Shops are open most of the day."

"No. But let's do what you said on the Sunday instead."

Frustratingly, Charlotte was not willing to make love that night. Which made it all the harder for him to get to sleep.

*   *   *   *   *   *

On Saturday, Charlotte left mid-morning and expected to be home by teatime. David was left to wonder whether he was merely suffering from the jealousy that had plagued his earlier relationships. It hadn't been a problem with her up to now, though; she was so loving, so committed, so desirable.

Could she possibly be deceiving him? The idea kept gnawing at his mind. He thought about phoning Bella's mobile on the pretext of asking about the wedding, but wondered if it might betray his fear. Or simply calling Charlotte. Instead, he phoned his brother to talk it through. Richard was an intelligent, moral man, a wine-drinking mate, and a good listener.

Richard sounded surprised, and was a little short, saying only that Bella was at home cooking something special for dinner later, and that he was on his way to the supermarket. It was a few moments before David registered the sound of a number of people chattering in the background. A pub, or maybe a restaurant. Oh God. It couldn't be, just couldn't.

Pacing around the house, and right out of character, in Charlotte's absence he couldn't resist the thought of taking a quick look in the drawers where she kept her paperwork. Shopping with Bella had seemed a natural thing to do at a weekend, so why did he see it as a piece in the jigsaw which was now making up a picture of Charlotte that he did not recognise.

Since they shared out the household bills between them, he was not surprised to find a neat pile of gas accounts and some large-scale supermarket shopping receipts. Then a mobile call account, and wait – a second account in her name, for a different number. Why hadn't she told him that she had two phones? He looked at the page listing calls on the account he recognised. Some of the numbers were known, family and friends and his own, but there was no pattern to the others and so nothing to raise any doubt.

The other account was different, and dated from just a couple of months ago. The calls were mostly to the same, unrecognised number, and David felt nausea and fear. Still, at least that cleared Richard, and he felt ashamed of the scenario he'd constructed.

Heart pounding, he poured himself a drink, draining the bottle, and sat down to look for an explanation. He went over what scant evidence he could find, but especially the fact that Bella was at home, *so where was Charlotte?*

* * * * * *
*

That evening, there was an atmosphere. Was he just imagining that Charlotte couldn't look him in the eye? Again he reached for a whisky, but the bottle was empty and there was no other. Struggling for self-control, he followed her into the kitchen, clutching the empty bottle.

"Good day shopping with Bella?"

"Yes thanks. Not that we found that special outfit for her, but we had lunch and wandered around the mall."

"You were definitely with Bella, then?"

She looked hard at him. "Why do you ask?"

"For Christ's sake, Charl. I *know* you weren't."

He raised the bottle and hurled it to the floor where it smashed by her feet.

In silence she fetched the dustpan and brush and cleared up the glass, right down to the tiniest shards. As tears began to form in his eyes, tears of rage, jealousy, fear, she placed the glass wordlessly in the bin and went to bed. He collapsed into a chair, dropped his head in his hands, and cried for the first time in three years.

The next day, Sunday, he was up early. Heading for the top floor of the house, he went to Charlotte's Moorcroft collection and picked out the largest, most flamboyant piece. In the kitchen he wrapped the precious piece in a tea towel, kicked down on it with his heel to start the destruction, then ground the pieces more finely under his shoe. He decanted them into a supermarket bag and took them carefully to a little-used cupboard.

Once she was up, they acted formally, like strangers, and the plan for a day out was not mentioned. That afternoon, though, he went to find her in the garden.

"Look, Charl. I'm sorry. I just don't understand. Please tell me what's going on." She assured him, nothing.

"OK then. What do you say we cook up a special dinner tonight and talk it through? You can tell me where you really were yesterday, and I can tell you what's on my mind."

It was agreed. David was a great cook, and he decided on an asparagus and goat cheese tart with perhaps a New Zealand Sauvignon that she'd like, and chocolate mousse with a glass of port. He found the Sauvignon in the cellar and chilled it. A last desperate hope that he was wrong and that the situation could be saved.

The food was ready on time, she laid the table, and he served the tart. They sat opposite one another and sipped their wine. Soon their plates were empty; she had taken only a small helping. He shared the last of the wine between them.

"I know about your second phone."

Her hand shook, spilling a few drops of wine. "How did you find out?"

She was furious to hear that he'd looked through her private papers. The temperature rose and both started flinging insults. Shouting, he accused her of lying, of seeing someone else. Calmly she replied that he was paranoid, not trusting her, imagining things that weren't true. But she did not actually deny it.

He became more subdued, and started to speak of everyday, unimportant things. Then he told her that he had a surprise for her in the cellar, to say sorry, and invited her to go and look while he served the mousse. She rose and went to the cellar door. He listened. She opened the door, switched on the light, and started down the steps into the cool, damp and musty room. The next moment he was behind her, pushing her forward before slamming the door and drawing the bolt. As she tumbled over and over downwards, the sharp shards of the Moorcroft pot that he'd scattered pierced her face, arms and legs while the hard edges of the steps cracked her ribs and broke a leg. As her head cleared, she screamed and shouted for him to come and let her out. Words he had never before heard her use – she was full of surprises. After a minute or two she struggled over to the nearest rack of wine to try and pull herself up. He heard the crash of bottles hitting the stone floor as the rack toppled. Wincing but determined, he picked up the car keys and his phone, and went to the off-licence to buy more Scotch.

Parked in a lay-by in the dark, he drank a good half of the bottle, then called Richard, not sure even now what he would say to him but to ask for help. Richard could tell that he'd been drinking, and dissuaded David from driving over to their house. Then the phone went dead, and David fell asleep across the front seats of his car.

At dawn he woke, but waited until eight to call Richard again and apologise. He asked if he would come over for dinner in a week's time, just him – no need to involve Bella - to talk over a particular problem and discuss how to solve it.

David drove home, parking a few yards away from the house, and let himself in silently. He listened but could hear no sound. Duly washed and in a suit he packed a suitcase and left for work, feeling nothing except for a blinding headache. He booked himself into a small local hotel for a couple of weeks.

*   *   *   *   *   *

A week later he returned home shortly before his brother was expected. The house was silent. He laid the table for two, poured a large whisky, and waited.

"Join me in a drink before dinner, Richard? Then I'll tell you what's on my mind."

Several drinks later, he began cautiously, saying Charlotte was behaving oddly. Then he confided that he suspected she might be seeing someone. They were both starting to slur their speech, though Richard was not saying much as yet.

"What's going on, Rich? I mean, has Bella said anything?" There was a pause.

"So Charlotte's told you about us?"

Then it came tumbling out. Richard said how he had always liked Charlotte, fancied her even on the quiet. David was motionless, waiting. He did not take his eyes off his brother.

"We met in town one day and had coffee. Then, you know how it is, one thing led to another. I bought a second phone, and so did she." David didn't know, hadn't ever been unfaithful. But here was the evidence he had been dreading, from a source he had considered but dismissed.

"You cheating, lying bastard. You mean it's *you*?"

Richard tried to calm him. Said it was over, had been only a couple of times. He was so sorry and would give anything to turn back the clock. Clearly he was lying, but he did admit that he'd tried to call Charlotte but she hadn't been answering her phone.

"Is she OK, Dave? I've been worried."

"As far as I know, yes. Probably a signal problem - she's been away all week on a walking trip with friends."

"Maybe, but still."

"Look, I need something else to drink, Rich, to take this all in. Why don't you nip down to the cellar and bring up a couple of bottles. Your choice. We've both always been wine freaks, and I'm sure you'll find something you love down there. I'll get the dinner."

Surprised but grateful that David was taking this bombshell so well, so far at least, Richard did what he'd been asked. He thought it odd that the light was already on, but had started down the steps when he felt a violent push from behind, sending him crashing down to land on the hard stone floor. The remnants of ceramic cut into his skin as he fell. At the bottom, he was just conscious enough to notice the light being switched off and to hear the cellar door slamming shut and he shouted, swore and cried out, to be met with silence.

Picking himself up gingerly, feeling the pain, he started to crawl back towards the steps. His hands and knees felt the slashing of smashed glass on the floor, then a wetness that he thought from the odour must be wine. Maybe some bottles had fermented – Dave kept them long enough down there. He remembered that a torch was kept at the bottom of the steps, and so, terrified and in agony, he reached for it and pressed the button.

First he looked in horror at the blood on his skin and clothes then, on seeing the spreadeagled, open-eyed body of Charlotte, bloodied, skin shredded, lying on broken glass in a pool of red wine, he screamed in shock, horror and fear, and passed out.

David washed their glasses and put them away. He repacked his bag, picked up the car keys, and drove to the off-licence and on to the hotel for the second week of his booking. He would sleep well that night.

THE DISAPPOINTING TALE OF SOUR PETER

It doesn't take a genius to guess how Sour Peter got his name.

No-one in the village knew how old he was, not even Peter himself, and his birth did not appear in the parish records so he can't have been local. Some guessed sixty, others much older since it must have taken decades and a multitude of fortune's slings and arrows for him to become such a gnarled, miserable and mean old man.

To give an example, there was only one time, that anyone could remember, when he'd given anything to anyone. He'd been trudging back to his scruffy, rundown lodgings when a young woman bravely stood in front of him holding out a box.

"Collecting for the poor, good sir." She was ready to dodge if he went for her. But two of the locals overheard, and stopped to witness what they thought would be another stream of invective from the old man. They, however, later vouched for the fact that he took a silver coin from his pocket and dropped it into the box. No-one knew why, and speculation was rife. Had he been wealthy in happier times? Had he just come into some money and kept the knowledge to himself? Or could the comeliness of the young lady have made him forget himself? All they knew was that, as he dropped in the coin, he was heard to mutter,

"There you are, Annie girl. That's for your poor. Now be off."

Annie was known locally as a good, kind and god-fearing young woman who had lived on her own since her mother died. She kept a tiny but clean house, lived modestly, and paid for her groceries on the nail. She earned just about enough by doing laundry for the better-off people who lived in large houses just outside the village, and mending shirts and petticoats for those who couldn't afford to buy new. The results of her occasional fundraising efforts were always given to the poorest people who had no income and no skills to earn any.

Following the silver coin incident, it did not go unnoticed that Sour Peter often happened to be hobbling along the roadside when Annie was returning home from collecting laundry from the outsiders. Although she was easily the more fit, once in a while he would offer to help carry some of her load as far as her door. He seemed to carry on conversations at times, but no-one could catch what was said, however hard they tried. And they did try.

In time, she started to invite him in, and he would disappear for a few minutes before emerging with various very small packages under his arm. Probably half a loaf, or even a cake, they thought.

Peter's visits to Annie became more regular and were lasting longer. The locals swore they could hear the occasional rough chuckle as well as the tinkling laugh they knew well, and the 'friendship' became the talk of the village.

Then the scandal – it seemed to the others that *Sour Peter had moved in with Annie*! The more generous said they hoped it would make him a more friendly, approachable figure but the less kind thought it a shocking thing to happen and they worried for Annie's immortal soul. Either way, Sour Peter's already ramshackle home was going to rack and ruin and no-one wanted it or thought it worth saving.

Annie was seen less and less around the village. She did her shopping in fewer trips with bigger loads, reduced the money collection rounds, and was less ready to offer sewing skills to her previous customers. Sour Peter himself was rarely seen, but they knew he was still there because his croaking voice and rasping cackle could still be heard.

Then some shock news spread quickly around the village. First, another young woman had been collecting and delivering the laundry from the outsiders. And not only that – Annie's alms to the poor seemed to have dried up, leaving them fretting about their next meals, not to mention their futures. And yet, said the villagers, we're sure she's been out collecting. One of the previous beneficiaries plucked up the courage to knock on Annie's door. She'd had to swallow her pride and asked if, by any chance, there had been donations recently that could help her out with some food for the children. Annie's curt reply shocked all who heard about it.

After a day or two, one of the village elders decided to investigate. He knocked on the door and asked Annie if she could mend a tear in his best shirt, since she had sewed other garments for him quite beautifully in the past. When the door opened, the elder tried to peer into the house; as he saw Sour Peter in an armchair he could smell the smoke from a pipe. When Annie realised he was prying, she slammed the door.

Soon, Annie was haggling with the shopkeepers to try to reduce their prices, and the gossips whispered that she was starting to develop unflattering lines on her once-lovely face. The draper caught her trying to push a couple of reels of cotton into her basket without paying, too. And when one of the village girls stopped her to ask for a contribution to the orphans' fund, she sailed past without replying. How different to the old, generous and friendly Annie.

Then, one day, a crowd started to gather around the house as word spread that the undertaker was about to call. A cheap pine coffin was borne in, and the door closed behind it. Everyone held their breath - they had no idea which of the two occupants was named on the box, and of course it would not be proper to ask. They would just have to keep their eyes open and wait.

Three days later, the undertakers returned and the coffin was slowly and solemnly carried out and placed on a cart. It was evidently heavier than when it went in – but perhaps not by much. And behind it came … Sour Peter. There was a collective gasp.

Poor Annie was buried in the churchyard with most of the villagers watching from a distance. Sour Peter, seemingly quite calm, threw a handful of soil onto the coffin and the reverend made the shortest of speeches. Then the curious group parted to let Peter through, but remained silent. They waited for him to reach the late Annie's house and shut the door behind him, then they slowly edged nearer until some were just a yard or two from the window. They heard the unmistakeable sound of the raucous chuckle, followed by a strange song that was almost merry in nature. One of the villagers dared to peer in through the window, to see a gnarled old man dancing a jig around Annie's old kitchen table.

RETRIBUTION

OK, yeah, I did do it. But there were reasons. And I sure as hell don't
> *deserve this.*

The straps are tightened, fastening his wrists, ankles, neck and thighs to the hard, plastic-sheeted gurney. The straps are starting to hurt; he tries to move his hands but that makes it worse, so he remains still.

He rolls his eyes to the side, and sees that his wife and his mother are clasping hands behind the glass.

I never meant to kill the kid, for Christ's sakes. I told them about our
> *precious Jessie, how she'd died the year before, and how that kid looked*
> *just like her. Rich brown curls, bright eyes and a smile to melt your heart.*
> *I only wanted to talk, to hold her hand. To feel close to Jessie again for*
> *just a moment. But she started screaming and wouldn't stop.*

The Velcro on the arm cuff snaps into place. The governor nods to the guard, who goes to stand by the door, then nods his head solemnly to signal to the doctor that it's time.

I mean, I've got kids of my own, for God's sake. What these people are doing
> *here is what you might call beyond revenge. Maybe they have kids that age.*
> *Maybe that's why. Wishing now that I hadn't refused the reverend.*

78

The doctor puts his black bag on the table and extracts the smaller of two syringes. He points it towards the ceiling and squirts a few drops out to remove air bubbles. It's not the first time he's done this, but still it's a human being.

They say the first one knocks you out, but gently. And that's it. You don't feel
the second. I hope to God they're right. Oh hell, she's looking right at me,
tears streaming down her face. She knows it's the last time – she shouldn't
have to suffer like this for what I did. Looks like she still loves me after all.

The syringe is emptied into his arm and the doctor steps back. His shoes squeak.

My mouth feels dry. I told them everything, said I'm sorry. Told her yesterday
how much I love her. Held her. She was allowed to bring the dog and I kissed
him. I can feel the cold sensation rushing up my arm. Can't see but I can hear
and thoughts are racing around my brain, all every which way.

The governor nods; the doctor approaches and sees closed eyes. He takes a larger syringe from his bag, pumps it into an arm that is trembling just slightly, and then places it carefully back in the bag. He glances at the clock, takes out his pen and notes down 09.35 on the form. Briefly time seems suspended. Nobody moves, not even behind the glass.

But wait. It's not how they told me. I'm starting to feel my hands again and I can just about see her. Starting to feel light, floating towards the glass; she's out of her seat, palms on the glass, mouth wide open in a silent scream..

Hey, here's a malfunction. I heard if it fails, they have to reprieve you to life. I'll make it right somehow, darlin'.

We'll be together again.

The doctor feels for a pulse. With his thumb he gently lifts an eyelid, looks to the governor and nods his head. The curtain slides across the glass, and they wheel the gurney away.

ROCKET

October 20th
All the family is gathered at the bedside, knowing that
death is just hours away. There's sadness of course, but
some lighthearted relief too, as the children ask naïve
questions and what time's lunch?

October 21st
Preparations for the funeral are already under way. There
is a letter of instruction, clear and unemotional, and
everyone is glad of it:
    No flowers.
    Donations to the local hospice.
    Use the local undertakers – the middle-aged man, not
the young lady who
        wears black fishnet tights and a short skirt and tries
not to smirk.
    Party after that!
    My ashes to be launched into space – if not too
expensive.

October 22nd
The envelope containing the will is opened. I stifle a
giggle at the bit about the 'bereaved partner' having to pay
for the party, but it's not generally considered funny. Most
faces reveal feelings about the way the estate is distributed
– but it all seems fair to me. The funeral is to be on
November 1st.

November 1st
All went according to plan; a good turnout and not too
much black. Although the days between death and the
funeral can be a sort of limbo, people have kept busy with
the plans for the event and for the wake, and letting
everyone know. The wake is muted but not sorrowful. The

ashes have been returned in a tasteful urn – no recyclable cardboard boxes, thank you.

November 4th
Forgive the pun, but the dust has more or less settled now and everyone is looking forward to the family fireworks party tomorrow. As a sort of 'life celebration', there's a rather expensive display planned, with the emphasis on massive noisy, brash rockets. The children seem to have forgotten the sadness, and everyone else is excited but trying not to appear too lighthearted because, you know.

November 5th
All the traditions are wheeled out. Potatoes baking on a metal tray at the edge of the bonfire, and cheers as the scruffy guy goes up. Hot soup in assorted mugs, held in gloved hands, and even toffee apples. The children grip sparklers just a little warily, and wave them in the air to make starry patterns – hearts, circles, initials. Then the fireworks begin. The contents of the urn have been sealed in a paper bag and attached to the biggest rocket; it will be the final firework of the evening, and the very last request will have been fulfilled. When it's time, the touch paper is lit and the group falls silent. With a fizz and a whoosh, the rocket soars upwards, after a few seconds exploding into showers of coloured sparks with a whining, whistling racket as they fall and fade.

Looking back, I didn't mind the funeral, and I really enjoyed the firework display, especially that last rocket of course. I must say, it felt good to grab a handful of my own ashes up here, and there aren't many that can say that.

They'd been together for three months when Dan suggested a holiday together. Bologna is nice in September, he said.

Jenna's heart leapt. Images formed of them strolling, arms entwined, through the shaded colonnades of that great, ancient Italian city, stopping for biscotti, drinking espresso and later Prosecco.

They trawled the lists of hotels and hostels on his laptop. He favoured value accommodation, as his student loan was not up to four-star level, but she wanted a good, central hotel and offered to pay some of his share since she was earning and had some savings. Eventually they agreed on Hotel Nico, leaving in six weeks' time, nicely placed on a side street off the Piazza Maggiore. Bed and breakfast for five nights seemed about right, as they could economise by taking wine and picnic food to their room for lunches and then eat out at night. The flights were reasonable, too, since they were easy about timings, and Jenna paid for them and for the hotel up front while he promised to write out a cheque for her when they got back and his account was back in the black.

"How do you know Bologna, Dan?"

"Oh, I went there for a short time before uni."

"On your own?" She held her breath.

"Not exactly. I'd met a student from there and she invited me to visit her. It was only for a two or three days, but I fell in love with the city straight away." She wondered if he'd fallen in love with anything other than the city, but dared not ask.

Over the next few days Jenna booked leave, and they chatted about things they might need to buy for their trip. They looked around department stores for what she teasingly called a 'man bag', which annoyed him a little, but then he caught sight of the large, yellow satchel in Men's Accessories. He ran his hand over the soft leather and put the satchel to his face to smell the unique scent of animal hide. Jenna knew this was the one.

"Dan, I'd love to buy it for you, if you'd let me."

He looked up suddenly, as if he'd been unaware she was there next to him. "It's not cheap, Jen." But he couldn't hide his eagerness.

She looked at the price tag, took a sharp breath and smiled. "And your point is?"

They hugged and the deal was done.

That evening, they talked about money. Dan admitted that he felt bad about letting her pay so much more than he had, at least in the short term, and she reassured him that all was well.

In the following days, though, almost imperceptibly things began to change. There had been minor irritations, which Jenna put down to her work stress and Dan's approaching final year at university. Then she found herself wanting to nag him about his untidiness and some frivolous spending on gig tickets and on nights out at the student bars with what he called his 'man group', a side swipe at her 'man-bag' tag. He accused her, once, of believing that her spending power gave her power over him and his life, and this turned her stomach. She remembered what her mother would often repeat: "What's said cannot be unsaid."

The crisis came when he picked up the yellow satchel and looped it across his body on the way out to a drinking session. She couldn't stop herself.

"Dan, do be careful with it. Drinks will stain it, and leather is so hard to keep clean. Why don't you save it for the holiday?"

He glared at her, a look as yet unfamiliar in their relationship. "Just because you paid for it, doesn't mean you can tell me how to use it. Or perhaps you'd like it back?" As her tears started to form, he was gone.

In the days that followed, Jenna realised that he would not be coming to Bologna. She tried to keep calm for work while making a decision about the trip. She felt cold and wretched, and couldn't imagine either the holiday alone or cancelling - although the booking was still valid and of course she'd told her family and friends. Eventually, after an evening of solo wine drinking at home, she came to her decision. She would cancel Dan's ticket, but her own and the hotel booking would stand. The warmth of Italy in September might lighten her heart and provide an exciting distraction. She bought a guide book.

The empty seat on the plane was a sad reminder; still, it was better than having to make small talk with a stranger, or have a business type nab the arm rest and rustle a broadsheet newspaper into the edge of her space.

The Hotel Nico was even better than its online details had suggested, and her room was fairly large for a city centre hotel and had everything she needed. The sun was hot and the area around the Piazza Maggiore was buzzing with students just starting their term. The city felt alive and friendly.

Some of the place names were a mouthful, but Jenna picked up a tourist map in the Piazza and found her way to the Palazzo dell'Archiginnasio where the Sala Anatomica was drawing the crowds. The university was the oldest in Italy, and was known almost from the start for its medical faculty; the Sala was the place to see waxworks fashioned around cadavers, as well as other gruesome models and specimens, and the dissection lecture theatre sent a chill down her spine.

As she sat on the bench around the central slab, an attractive dark-haired young woman came to sit next to her, evidently a student. They exchanged smiles.

"You are English, yes?"

"Si. How did you know?"

"We are good at identifying the different nationalities. And the English are especially interested in our medical rooms."

"The specimens next door made me feel a little sick, actually. Are you a medical student?"

"Si. And you know what we say? A cognac is the best cure for the sickness! Doctor Margherita says."

Before long, Jenna and Margherita were sitting outside a bar with an espresso and a slice of pizza each, and one brandy too. It needed only a little sympathy for Jenna's story to be told, but with her companion so lively and cheerful, she held back the tears. Margherita invited her to join a student group in a different bar – Maxim - that evening.

"I shall have something for you then."

"What is it?"

"You will see. Eight o'clock?"

The group were well into a cocktail when Jenna reached Maxim's, and they greeted her warmly and, laughing, ordered her a strawberry margherita. As she sipped it through the salt rim, the real Margherita handed her a tiny package and whispered,

"I said I'd bring something for you. Here, it will make you feel happy, for a while at least. We take these all the time – just look around the group and you can see. Take just one at a time."

There seemed no harm; the evening was warm, the company delightful, and the drink a real joy, so she put a pill in her mouth and swallowed it. It left no taste, and the chatter continued, some in English for her benefit. She felt herself starting to relax.

The colonnades were still full of people, mostly students, as Jenna made her way contentedly back towards Hotel Nico. But her calm was shattered as a flash of yellow ahead caught her eye. A young man appeared to be carrying a yellow satchel across his body, but he walked quickly and she could not catch up. She couldn't see him clearly, but had a sense that he was with someone dark-haired, arm around her shoulder, and then he was gone. Feeling foolish, she reached the hotel and settled for the night. Dan's was not the only satchel in the world. And apart from that incident, the pill seemed to be having a relaxing and cheering effect.

The next three days passed pleasantly in a haze of art-packed churches, bookshops and markets, and cafes crowded with students and locals. Jenna was managing a reasonable Italian vocabulary by now, and used it whenever she could.

Strolling along Via Zamboni towards the supermarket, she heard a call from behind her.

"Hey, Jenna!"

"Margherita! Buongiorno."

"Have you been taking your medicine?"

"Yes, and thank you. It seems to be helping."

"Good. See you at Maxim's this evening?"

Jenna had the pills in her bag, and after shopping for bread, cheese, fruit and water she took one with a caffe latte.

Later in the day, not far from the hotel, the flash of yellow was again ahead of her. This was troubling – she still could not see the wearer too well, but he was with what seemed to be the same young woman. Again she tried to weave her way along the colonnade, but lost them. Could it be Dan? And surely not … Margherita? Heart pounding, she ran to the hotel and up to her room. Two glasses of water later, she dropped onto the bed and tried to make sense of what she'd seen. She would not go to Maxim's that evening.

The last full day would be spent hunting for souvenirs and for gifts for her family and friends. By the evening, balsamic vinegar from the distillery in Modena weighed down her shopping bag, together with gift-wrapped chocolate bricks from Majani's, a delightful little shop in business since the late 18th century. Jenna wondered how the staff kept so slender – but then most Italians did, especially the young people, despite all the pizza, pasta and croissants. She had chosen an especially nice box of pralines for Margherita, to thank her for friendship and support, so she would need to get to Maxim's that evening. She took another pill – there were still a number left but perhaps no more would be needed after this.

The group in the bar, with a few new faces, were well established by the time she arrived. Margherita jumped up to wave, and Jenna went to her.

"I brought you something in return," she said softly. "I hope you like these."

Margherita was delighted. "Thank you, Jenna. It's your last night, yes? We shall miss you. What would you like to drink?"

By now Jenna could understand a fair amount of the conversation, and was even able to join in, if still tentatively. She was sad when the group started to break up, and they said their goodbyes.

And then, surely it couldn't be? The blasted yellow satchel and, yes, she was sure it was Dan. She called out.

"Dan! Wait! It's Jenna. Please wait." But he turned a corner and was gone.

Her head swimming from the drinks, she somehow got back to her room and, pillow damp with tears, fell into a disturbed sleep for her last night in Italy.

Back home, and alone, Jenna could not stop thinking about her trip – partly the group, the hotel, the food, the warmth, but largely the sighting of – what could it have been except Dan? Or was she slowly going mad? After a large glass of wine and in a surge of sadness and the sense of loss, she opened Margherita's packet again and looked at the nine pills remaining. On impulse she swallowed them all, lay on the sofa, and in a few minutes began to lose consciousness.

As she faded, the door opened. It was Dan, tousled and troubled.

"Jenna! Thank God you're back." When she could not focus on him, he realised she was sick. "What's the matter, Jen? Look, I felt awful after you went. I'd treated you so badly, and never told you that I loved you, although now I know that I do." Then he saw the empty packet from the hallucinogenic drug on the floor beside her and snatched it up, but it appeared nameless. He grabbed his phone and dialled for an ambulance; it arrived too late and she was gone. He kissed her forehead as they took her away, and slumped down onto the sofa in grief. His tears fell unnoticed onto the yellow satchel on his lap, leaving a mark just as she'd said.

Acknowledgements

Special thanks to John Pye for all his support during the writing and publishing of *Bottles and Pots*. He has known when to encourage, when to ask questions, and when to lie low!

I'd also like to thank all the members of Penny Legg's Southampton Writing Buddies. The group has been a continuing source of ideas, movitation and creative energy, and without them this book would still be in its planning stages, if that. Seeing others writing and publishing their work has helped me to believe that I could do that, too.

Contacting the Author

Website: http://www.jacpye.com
Twitter: @JacquelinePye

Made in the USA
Charleston, SC
29 September 2013